A desperate search

The cub started bawling again, his cry pitched with panic. Josh ignored it. He couldn't stop now, not for Pokey, not for the storm, not for anything.

Wind stung his eyes. Back and forth along the bouldered ridge he searched—where could he go? The biggest rocks stood alone, offering little protection. His strength had seeped from his body like water from a rusty bucket. Soon the bucket would be empty. And then what?

BEN MIKAELSEN

RESCUE

JOSH McGUIRE

HYPERION PAPERBACKS FOR CHILDREN
NEW YORK

© 1991 by Ben Mikaelsen.
Printed in the United States of America.
For information address Hyperion Books for Children,
114 Fifth Avenue, New York,
New York 10011.

SCHOOL BOOK CLUB EDITION

Library of Congress Cataloging-in-Publication Data
Mikaelsen, Ben
Rescue Josh McGuire / Ben Mikaelsen — 1st ed.
p.   cm.
Summary: When thirteen-year-old Josh runs away to the mountains of
Montana with an orphaned bear cub destined for laboratory testing,
they both must fight for their lives in a sudden snowstorm.

ISBN 0-7868-1041-6

[1. Bears — Fiction.   2. Wildlife rescue — Fiction.   3. Runaways — Fiction.
4. Survival — Fiction.   5. Montana — Fiction.]   I. Title.
PZ7.M5926Re   1991   [Fic] — dc20   91-71386   CIP   AC

I WOULD LIKE TO DEDICATE THIS BOOK TO:

My wife, Melanie — *I love you.*

Dr. Philip R. Sauer — Who taught me how potent words could be. Also that a canoe ride is more important than a board meeting.

Richard S. Wheeler — Whose wisdom and encouragement I treasure.

Sandra Choron — A special agent and friend who believed in me.

Buffy — A 600-pound black bear who taught me to have respect and be gentle.

CHAPTER CHAPTER 1

THE BEAR appeared among the aspen, gliding ghostlike toward the crystalline mountain stream. Her young cub lingered behind, romping about in the underbrush, bounding, spinning, and tumbling. Overhead, chickadees flitted branch to branch, their two-tone songs hushed by the soft wind whispering through the treetops.

Like a thunderclap, a rifle shot split the crisp spring air. Back and forth across the steep ravine the sound echoed and then hung, gradually dissipating and leaving the narrow valley blanketed in uneasy silence.

Down beside the stream, the black bear sow stumbled in midstride—she tried to catch herself but fell headfirst into the shallow cold water. She had come to drink and to rest and to let her only cub splash. Now, failing to recapture life with one last mighty breath, she lay still.

Thirteen-year-old Josh McGuire crouched behind a log forty yards upslope from the water. Wide eyed, he stole a glance up at his father, Sam, who firmly lowered his rifle.

"Got him!" Sam muttered.

Josh breathed fast, the thunderous rifle shot echoing in his mind. He nodded as his father started toward the bear.

"You stay put," Sam said over his shoulder. "I'll go see if he's down for good."

"Dad," Josh asked weakly. "Why don't you wait in case he's not dead? That's what you always—"

"Shut up!" Sam said and kept moving.

Josh puzzled. Dad always told him you should wait before going up to a downed animal—especially a bear. Once they sat for two hours waiting on a downed elk. That time it had been fun, sitting with Dad, joking and telling stories—swapping lies, his dad called it. Glancing down now, Josh stared at the empty whiskey bottle lying in the grass.

His father stumbled toward the stream, muscles rippling and bulging under a faded orange shirt. The shirt, once bright and visible a ridge away, had been stained often by animal blood. Of late, spilled whiskey also made its mark.

Josh waited, staring at the black mound stretched motionless in the narrow mountain stream. The bear had seemed so much bigger when it was still alive and moving through the trees, its head tilted back, drifting warily side to side.

When Sam reached the bear, he tensed, reaching with a stick to poke it. His rifle was in position to fire.

Upstream, a small black animal scampered into some deadfall trees. The movement caught Josh's eye. "Dad, I saw a cub upstream," he shouted. "Did you shoot its mom?"

Sam only turned with an icy stare, deliberately motioning for Josh to come.

Josh ran up. "Did you see him, Dad? Dad, did you?"

Sam grabbed out, his grip biting into Josh's thin arm. Josh grimaced—he hated to show hurt in front of anybody. Sam spun him around. "Boy, you ever holler again when I'm poking a downed critter, I'll whup you till you're black as this here bear. Understand me?" he snapped.

Josh nodded, painfully aware of his mistake.

"Now, get the packs and give me a hand skinning," Sam ordered.

Rubbing his shoulder, Josh was glad he hadn't cried. He hated seeing anyone cry. His brother, Tye, had seldom cried, except after getting a rare licking. And even those lickings seemed to be for things that were funny. Josh remembered Tye's antics.

Once Tye came in the house after helping pull calves during calving season. Without washing his hands, he reached in and sneaked a couple of cookies from the cookie jar. That night Mom got furious. Not so much because Tye stole a couple cookies, but because he left afterbirth on the rest.

Another time, Pastor Woodward from the church paid a visit to their ranch. Right off, Tye took the overweight man down by the stream. Josh couldn't believe his eyes. Tye led the pastor across the old log.

Tye knew the old log was rotten, and using it to cross the stream had become a risky game. Like a cow being led to slaughter, Pastor Woodward followed Tye dutifully out across the log. Tye made sure he rushed ahead to be clear of the weak log when the man's weight sent him crashing into the stream. Boy did Tye get a thumping for that one.

"Hurry up!" Sam roared, jolting Josh from his daydreaming.

He rushed to retrieve the packs, the whole while watching upstream for the cub. Already Sam had the bear dragged from the water. Blood gurgled from a matted neck wound and puddled brightly among the new spring grass and rotted leaves.

Josh dropped the packs. "Is this the cub's mom?" he asked, voice shaking.

Sam swore. "I reckon it's a sow, but she's no mother." Irritation thickened his words. "You didn't see a cub. This she-bear's dry . . . dry as kindling." He reached out his bloody hand and pinched one of the big teats. A foamy white substance leaked out easily. Sam coughed and his voice got hard. "That's not milk," he said.

Josh knew not to argue with his father. But still he glanced over his shoulder as he helped skin back the heavy black pelt. Had Dad shot a mother bear? That was against the law if she had a cub. Maybe it was only a rock chuck or a porcupine that ran. Dad never shot anything he shouldn't or said anything he didn't believe—not until a year ago, anyway.

Soon only a meaty skeleton, a gut pile, a big stack of bloody slabbed meat, and a crumpled pelt remained. Sam wrapped the pelt in terry cloth and lowered it into a pack. "See if that's too heavy for you," he ordered.

Josh shouldered the load. It pinched his thin bony shoulders, but he tried to be casual. "Naw, shouldn't be no problem," he said, knowing they were a thousand feet up from the meadows of Tom Miner Basin and two miles from the truck. But he wanted so bad to make his father proud—a task that seemed to grow harder and harder.

It hadn't always been this way. Not until last year during hunting season. His older brother, Tye, had asked to go with Dad on a sheep hunt in the Spanish Peaks. Dad refused because he said this was a hunting trip just for the men—this was a trip with his hunting buddies. Next year, he promised, he would take Tye and Josh.

Next year never got the chance. That weekend with Sam gone, Tye was killed in a car accident on a gravel road west of town—he didn't see a sharp turn in the dark.

It hadn't been Dad's fault—Tye was probably driving crazy. So why did Dad blame himself? After the accident, Dad started drinking more and more. He insisted Josh come along on every hunting trip. This last year, nothing Josh did pleased his father. He was only thirteen—too short, too weak, and too stupid. Tye had been in high school and played football. Dad always bragged about Tye.

Josh longed for the old days when they all saddled the horses and raced each other lickety-split up to the county road and back. But now Tye was gone, and his father grew more and more angry. At home Dad had started yelling at Mom. He never used to yell at her. In fact they used to get mushy all the time. He would tickle her, and she would tie his shoelaces together. Then they would hug and kiss. Now Sam swore and gave Josh lickings—and the lickings grew sharper. Would he ever make his father happy? Be his buddy? Be like Tye?

As the sun arched higher in the June sky, it warmed the thin air. Sam stuffed the bags of bloody meat into his pack, then headed out across the ravine toward the ridge. Josh noticed his father's walk was unsteady—this wasn't like him. Sam's friends nicknamed him Billy Goat for his sure footing.

"Are you coming?" Sam rumbled.

Josh scrambled after him, wrinkling his nose at the sweet putrid smell of the gut pile—by tomorrow it would flat out stink! Reaching the ridge, Josh struggled under his load. As the trail steepened and angled down across loose shale, Josh stumbled and fell to his knees, scraping his leg. Blood trickled down inside his pants, but he said nothing.

Something bothered Josh. He had never seen his father breathe and sweat as hard as today. Even ten-mile hikes off Buffalo Horn Pass had not caused the heavy beads of sweat now glinting on Sam's forehead.

Slowly Josh's legs numbed and turned leaden. He

blinked at the stinging sweat in his eyes. His tongue clogged his throat like a dry rock. For another half hour he wobbled forward, with each step fighting back at the big invisible hand that pulled him harder toward the ground.

Finally Sam called a halt. "What's wrong, Joshua—need an elevator? I'd never guess you were Tye's brother."

The words cut Josh deeper than any shale.

"Here, give me your pack," Sam said.

Josh nodded silently, his heart hammering and lungs burning—he had neared his limit no matter what they did. When his father looked away, he quickly wiped sweat from his forehead with a sleeve. He also unbuttoned the front of his shirt to cool down. Ashamedly he looked down at his skinny white chest and washboard ribs. He didn't have very big muscles, not like his dad's brawny, powerful build.

Next Josh glanced back up the mountain. He was haunted by the memory of the black furry animal he'd seen bound into the trees. What if it was a cub? And what if they had shot its mom?

"Let's go," Sam said.

When they started again the going was much easier. But seeing Sam carry the extra pack like a suitcase brought a lump to Josh's throat—he hadn't done his share. The rest of the way he blinked back tears, watching his dad labor under all the weight. A two-hour hike off the mountain had taken most of the afternoon.

When finally they reached camp, Sam iced the

meat and pelt in a cooler, then started fixing supper. Josh hurt and felt faint, but at least he'd gotten his wind back. No longer did his mouth feel caked with powder. The setting sun made the air brisk. Quickly Josh started collecting firewood before his father ordered him to.

Sam had started supper. A cast-iron skillet rested between three big rocks, absorbing heat from a bed of glowing coals. Beside the fire pit Josh spotted the ever-present bottle. Already Sam took long drawn-out guzzles. Soon he would be angry no matter what happened. Why did his father get so angry? Why did he drink so much?

Josh knew it wasn't because the whiskey tasted good. One night when no one was home, Josh had opened up the bottle and taken a gulp. The whiskey stung his mouth, burning deep into his ears and face. He actually touched his face to see if it was hot. That couldn't be what his father enjoyed.

After gathering wood, Josh tried to ward off Sam's impending anger. "You know, Dad, it's never taken me more than one match to start a fire," he said.

Sam glared, rocking the bottle loosely. "What do you mean? I've seen you waste half a box sometimes."

"Nope," Josh insisted. "Never have. Maybe I used a bunch before one worked, but it only took one." He chuckled at his own wit until he saw the blank stare on his father's face. Josh quit talking. Why couldn't it be like old times?

It used to be the four of them: Mom and Dad, and Tye and himself. Together they laughed and joked until the wee hours of the night. Once out camping, Tye put minnows in Dad's canteen. When Dad pulled a live minnow from his mouth, everybody, including Dad, rolled on the ground and pounded the grass with laughter. If Josh did that now, he'd get a good walloping.

"Josh," Sam spit. "Get some water."

Josh grabbed a small bucket and ran to the stream. He dipped carefully into a clear pool, avoiding sediment—a little was unavoidable. When he returned, his father looked into the bucket skeptically. "Tye always brought back water as clean as from a spigot," he said. "You'd bring back mud if you thought I wouldn't notice."

It wasn't so, Josh thought. Why did Dad say things like that? He'd learned not to answer back, though. He'd learned real quick.

"What's wrong? Turkey got your tongue?" Sam asked.

Josh hung his head silently.

After supper Josh picked up the dishes and limped to the stream. The raw scrape on his leg had matted his pant leg with blood. Dad hadn't even noticed—he sat by the fire, rolling the whiskey bottle back and forth in his fingers. Already a glazed look filled his eyes, and Josh knew to avoid it.

Finishing the dishes, Josh set them carefully under a tree and worked his way downstream. Soon it would be dark—and safe to return to camp. Then Dad would be passed out beside the fire or asleep in the pickup camper.

Memories of this day made Josh want to cry. He sat on a smooth rock overlooking a short section of ripples. Two squirrels chased each other helter-skelter through nearby trees, their angry chattered insults spilling from among the branches. Josh eased off his pants and lowered his scraped knee into the icy water. Gently he rubbed the tender skin and let the current numb away the pain. Traces of blood leaked like a red string into the stream.

After putting his pants back on, he stared at his shimmering, broken reflection in the ripples. Then his eyes wandered to the hills above the campground. Was there a young cub up there somewhere without a mom? If there was, it would wander for days bawling for its mother and hurting from hunger. After that it would die. No one would know. This weighed on Josh's mind. He tried to doubt his memory. Had he really seen a cub? Yes! Yes, he had! And his father had orphaned it.

CHAPTER 2
CHAPTER

JOSH STAYED by the stream long after dark. At last he slipped into the camper. Raspy breathing and snores rumbled from the top bunk. Josh squirmed out of his clothes and crawled in below.

As long as Josh could remember, his father had tucked him into bed at night. Even as Josh grew older Dad would come to the room and say good-night as if bidding farewell to a traveler. He spoke of sleep as if it were a great adventure, a journey into the unknown.

Josh could still hear Dad's voice saying, "Josh, you must go now and sleep with the angels. They're waiting, and you mustn't disappoint them. I'll see you when you come back in the morning. Then you can tell me everything you've seen. But go now—hurry! Go and sleep with the angels." The anticipation glowing on Dad's face was the most wonderful farewell.

But tonight, and during the last year, Dad had not bid farewell as usual. Nor would Josh go to sleep with the angels tonight. Instead, thoughts of the cub boiled in his head. Was the little bear huddled somewhere, alone and scared, bawling for its mother, and for her milk?

Josh tried to shake away the thoughts, but even after hours of tossing and turning, he could not. Maybe he could sneak up and catch it. Even if it meant a good licking, he couldn't let the cub die. If he did dare go after the cub, should he leave a note? It might make Dad more mad.

At last, Josh edged from his bunk. Darkness masked his skinny body, but not the hurt in his leg. He stifled a yawn and tried to rub the night's drowsiness from his eyes. Two thoughts hung in his head like signs, too big to be ignored: somewhere up the mountain was a cub he had to save, and if he did, his father would get mad. The thoughts shoved at each other.

After scooping up his crumpled clothes, he fumbled around for a flashlight. Also a pencil and paper. Then he stole into the cold night.

He shivered, squirming into his flannel shirt and dirty, ripped jeans. Then, with the small flashlight held awkwardly in his teeth, Josh hesitated. All of his thoughts about the cub, about his dad, about Tye, all the notions that kept him awake half the night, they hunkered down in his tired mind. But before he could chicken out, he scribbled:

Dear Dad—Please don't get mad.
I went to get the cub. I'll be back fast.
                                        Josh

———

Josh crawled back inside the camper and left his note on the table, tucked under the edge of the whiskey bottle—Dad couldn't miss it. Quietly he pulled a small daypack from the closet and paused in the dark. What would he need?

First he stuffed in a length of rope and a big bag of his mom's oatmeal cookies. Dad wouldn't understand feeding the cookies to a bear, but Mom would, and she made them. To ward off the morning's chill, he grabbed his heavy down jacket. If the day broke sunny, the jacket might get too hot. But early June weather in the high country could also turn nasty.

Josh stared up at the shadow of his sleeping father. This was stupid—he ought to forget this foolishness and go back to bed. Swallowing hard, he slipped into the cold air and squeezed the door closed behind him.

A half-moon dipped low in the night sky, casting little light. It had to be getting close to sunrise—he needed to get going. Shouldering his light pack, he headed toward the hills. His muscles ached and he favored his gashed leg.

The shapes of trees, logs, and boulders moved past, hulking in moon shadow like hidden people and crouched animals. Josh squinted to pick his footing. Leaving the normal trail, he cut across the lower meadow and up a narrow ravine. Branches grabbed at his jacket, and several times deadfall sent him sprawling. If he didn't get lost, or hurt, this shortcut should save almost an hour.

He hiked in a sea of black, alert to every sound.

The trickling sound of water melted past in the night. Far to the north coyotes yipped shrilly to each other. Overhead a restless wind rustled through the leaves, and a crashing sound faded away into the trees— probably a surprised deer.

Josh liked the dark. Even when he was much younger he enjoyed wandering out away from the ranch house at night. He'd perch on a large mound of field rocks and look back. The house and yard glowed clearly.

One night he saw his brother, Tye, silhouetted in the lighted doorway. Josh hollered, "Hey, Tye!" But Tye stood blindly peering out into the night, not sure where the call came from. Again Josh called, "Hey, Tye!" Still his brother gazed off in the wrong direction. It was a wonderful discovery; if you were part of the darkness, you were invisible—you were its friend.

Josh paused to glance down the ravine and to slow his breathing. Cold air from a mounting breeze nipped at his cheeks and seeped down his neck. Josh fumbled with the zipper and worked the collar up around his ears. Maybe he should turn back. If he did, his father might not even know he'd left. Would the cub's death be his fault if he didn't try to help? Deliberately he pressed on.

Nearing the ridge, a hint of light touched the horizon. Still the mountains loomed dark and menacing ahead. It was less than a half-hour hike now to where he had spotted the cub. He needed to hurry. If the cub slept near where the mother died, it would be frantically hungry and might soon wander. Josh climbed the ridge until he recognized the steep ravine dropping off to his right. Now the eastern horizon glowed lush red, and snow started falling.

Josh could see only clear sky glinting through the flakes that drifted down big and soft as feathers. Some snow might help if he had to track the cub, but any more could spell trouble—all he wore was sneakers.

As quickly, the snow turned to icy sleet. Thick clouds fogged the mountain, hiding familiar landmarks. Josh's cheeks and hands stung as he dropped into the trees for shelter. At last he recognized the kill site and slowed to a near standstill. Overhead, dawn seeped through the curtain of fog. Eyeing the sky, Josh guessed the sun was now up. The air breathed crisp and misted when he exhaled.

He stepped cautiously, placing each foot to avoid branches or twigs. Every few yards he stopped and listened, letting his eyes wander and skip about. A forest had noises even when it was quiet. It had noises that said everything was okay, and it had noises that said something was wrong. This morning Josh wasn't sure what the sounds were saying.

As he spotted the gut pile near the stream, the sleet stopped, and a pale patch of blue sky moved like a ghost in the clouds. The dusting of snow was fast melting. Josh looked closer now, smelling a rank odor. The guts were scattered, and the reddish, gristle-covered bones were strewn about.

He panicked. Coyotes! They always scavenged the remains of any kill. Had they found the cub? Josh breathed fast. He scanned the ground beyond the bones and intestines until he spotted a light patch of earth some twenty feet to his left. He rushed to the patch and knelt. Two small tracks pushed deep into the soft ground. Josh's breathing stopped short and he blinked. Dad had taught Tye and him to read many kinds of tracks—he said some day their life might depend on it. Of all tracks, the most exciting was bear. Looking down, Josh smiled. It was the cub!

He removed his pack and slid out the rope, tying a loop in one end and feeding the other end through to make a noose. Then he stuffed his pockets with cookies, passing up the urge to eat one. Dim shadows cloaked the nettled forest floor. The cub, if it was around, would be scared and probably run.

Josh inched slowly, examining every tree and mound. Nothing. If the cub strayed, then it could be anywhere and chances of finding it were slim. Still nothing moved. All that showed were his own footprints. Icy dew was numbing his toes—he couldn't give up. He focused on a big deadfall tree about sixty feet from the gut pile. It angled sideways and might allow the cub protection.

Silently he approached, searching the ground inch by inch. There were no tracks. Unconsciously he drew in a long breath and held it until his lungs burned. Then, breathing out slowly, he neared the deadfall. Carefully he bent over, using one hand to lower his chest to the big log. He swept his eyes back and forth—still, nothing.

As he tensed to push himself upright again, he spotted a small clump of black hair, nearly within arm's reach. It was tucked deep under the log and Josh had to lean completely across to see it clearly. Staring straight into his face, not two feet away, were two glassy, black button eyes.

CHAPTER 3
CHAPTER

THEY STARED at each other, motionless. Josh held his breath. Even the wind stood still. The cub crouched under the log, shivering, its big claws clutching the ground. Woolly black hair covered its body with a kinky soft pile. Big ears perked sharply upward from a tiny, innocent face.

Suddenly the cub bolted for the clearing, front paws pumping out from under its fuzzy rump. Josh stood to give chase but then stopped, crawling slowly over the log and dropping to the ground. If he gave chase the cub's fear would override its hunger, and Josh might never catch it.

At the edge of the clearing the cub stopped, looking back. Josh waited. He knew cubs were born in hibernation, sometime late in January or early February. This cub must be at least four months old. It was bigger than the bum lambs at the farm—about the size of a large raccoon. And much more solid—probably twenty or twenty-five pounds.

Josh slipped out a cookie and tossed it gently toward the cub. Shivering, the animal glared back. Time ceased to exist, as did the sun and the sky and the trees, or any thought of Dad. All that existed was a scruffy frightened cub and a cookie only a few feet from its nose.

Slowly the cub twitched its nose higher in the air, blinking at the cookie. Then, trembling, it crept forward, stomach nearly touching the ground. Its gaze froze on the tempting disk in the grass. Grunting, it sprang forward, wolfing the sweet thing down with a gasping sound.

Before the cookie was swallowed, Josh threw another closer to himself. This time the cub barely waited before scampering forward. Several more cookies brought it within ten feet. Still it eyed Josh warily.

As the cub chewed and gulped on cookies, Josh draped the loop of rope between his knees—he had to coax the cub through it. To be safe, he tied the free end around his wrist. Then he flicked out small pieces of cookie with his thumb, like marbles.

The frightened cub scurried back and forth, coming closer and closer. Soon it came right up, sniffing and bobbing its head. Josh placed a big cookie between his legs so the cub would have to come through the loop. Barely hesitating, the cub dove for the cookie.

Josh yanked the rope hard, and the world exploded. Spinning frantically, the cub bawled and twisted, snugging the rope tight around its chest and snaring a front leg. Claws ripped and tore at Josh as the cub scrambled free. Before Josh could react, the cub bolted and hit the end of the line. This jerked Josh forward in the grass and tumbled the cub upside down, its stubby legs pawing the air. It rolled to its feet facing Josh. With a crazed bawl, it charged.

Josh winced as the angry bundle of black hit him. The cub's stubby milk teeth tore at his arm—harder even than his father's grip. Urgent grunts and snarls erupted as claws dug into Josh's shoulder, ripping his jacket.

Nothing had prepared Josh for the crazed attack. He closed his eyes and grabbed the cub with all his strength. He wrenched the twisting fireball out away from his body, with claws raking his wrists and arms.

"Dang you!" Josh screamed, fighting hard. He gripped the cub's neck, but a kick from its rear leg caught him between the thighs. The trees blurred, and his grip melted.

The cub spun, bolting again. The rope jerked, pulling Josh's wrist under him and nearly somersaulting him. His arm twisted hard, and his eyes watered. Doubled over, he clenched his teeth trying to bite away the pain. When Josh looked up, the cub cowered at its end of the rope, shaking, glaring, and blowing menacingly through curled lips.

Minutes passed before Josh could crawl to his feet. His jacket was shredded. Cautiously he slipped a hand inside his shirt to nurse his shoulder. Something felt wet, and he pulled his hand out to find blood on his fingers.

"I can't save you if you kill me," he mumbled.

The cub watched sullenly, still shaking.

"You bonehead," Josh muttered. "C'mon, let's go." He pulled hard on the rope and braced for another attack. The cub struggled on stiff legs, grunting with protest—but followed. Josh kept looking back as he walked. The cub might be small, but it didn't fight small.

CHAPTER 4

CHAPTER

AFTER REACHING the ridge, the cub trailed downhill more willingly. By then, however, it had earned the name Pokey. Every few minutes Josh turned and offered bits of cookie, coaxing, "Easy, little fella, easy now. Must be scared, huh? I would be if someone shot my mom . . . or dad." But nothing changed the cub's forlorn look.

Sweat burned at Josh's scrapes and cuts. Pausing, he stuffed his ripped jacket in the pack, then looked up. A shimmering sun hung in a vacant blue sky. Pokey had quit fighting and shivering, but still he sulked.

"We're almost there, Pokey," Josh encouraged. But Pokey plodded along, head hung low.

When they rounded the last bend, Josh spotted the pickup. Would Dad have found the note? He couldn't get mad once he saw the cub—now the cub was safe. The camper door stood open, no one in sight. Worry haunted Josh and he paused, sudden fear tugging at him. Why was he afraid? The cub would have died—wouldn't Dad see that? Besides, Dad hadn't said not to go after the cub—nor had he given permission. Did that make this right or wrong? Drawing in a deep breath, Josh ducked under a fallen tree on the trail and pulled the cub into camp.

"Dad," he called, hesitating.

A muffled thump followed the creaking of a bunk. Sam loomed onto the tailgate, shirt unbuttoned, hair tangled. He looked down with a dull stare.

Josh tried to smile but eyed the whiskey bottle in his father's left hand. "Dad, I found the cub," he stammered, limping forward. Dried blood caked his arms and neck. One pant leg was ripped.

Sam bellowed hoarsely, "You found a cub all right. A damn stupid thing to do."

Josh grimaced. "What do you mean?"

"The mother could have killed you—pulling a dumb stunt like that."

Josh looked down and swallowed hard. "Dad . . . the mom's dead. We shot her."

Sam leaped off the tailgate, fire in his eyes. "I told you we didn't shoot no mom. There's a sow up there now looking for this cub, and you, dumb fool, you're waltzing it into camp like you own it." Sam's loud voice and fast approach caused the cub to squall backward.

"But, Dad," Josh cried, "I found the cub sleeping right near the gut pile. He was—"

Sam's hand smashed across Josh's face like a baseball bat, snapping his head hard to the side. Thunder erupted in his ears and funny colors crawled across the sky. As he fell, all he could think to do was cling to the rope. A sweet taste filled his mouth and his eyes watered.

Sam reached down, trembling. "I . . . I didn't mean to hit you, Josh," he stammered. "I only meant to slap you."

Josh scrambled backward on his knees, everything blurring. "Get away from me! Get away from me!" he shouted, clawing at the ground. The cub twisted and jerked on the rope, helping pull Josh away. When his father's hazy form no longer loomed over him, Josh crouched. Dad had become a crazy man.

Sam's shoulders sagged and he stumbled around the front of the pickup. Suddenly he kicked the bumper, then lashed out, striking the hood with his bare fists, over and over. Josh watched, trembling. The cub struggled madly.

Sam returned with blood on his hands.

"Please don't hit me again, Dad, please," Josh pleaded.

"I'm not going to hit you, Son," Sam said, his eyes blinking and voice subdued. "Put the cub in the camper."

"Are we going home?"

Sam nodded.

Still nursing his cheek, Josh lifted the bawling cub into the camper with the rope. "I'm going to ride back here," he said, pulling the cub inside.

Sam walked over. "Josh . . ."

Josh refused to meet his father's gaze.

"Josh, I . . ." Sam paused, pressing a bloodied fist

against his lips. Then he turned and headed for the cab.

Bouncing and rattling down the road, Josh found grub for the cub. At first he eyed Josh with distrust, then ate and drank cautiously. Afterward he edged his woolly rump closer, peering up fearfully. Josh rested his hand on the cub's back and felt trembling under the soft fuzzy hair.

"Oh, Pokey, I'm so sorry for everything," Josh said. "We shouldn't have killed your mom. What are we going to do?"

The cub seemed to understand, pressing tightly against Josh, his eyes gleaming with fright.

Sam's actions hadn't made sense to Josh. Several times he remembered his father staying up all night at the ranch to save a calf or foal—even a puppy or kitten. How could he not care if the cub died?

After seven miles of rough gravel, they reached pavement and the rattling stopped. The tires hummed on the smooth highway, and warm sunlight flooded through the side window. Soon the cub nodded and closed his button eyes. Josh gently drew Pokey over on his lap with no fight.

Exhausted himself, Josh scarcely noticed the seventy-mile trip north through Paradise Valley and west over Bozeman Pass. The cub snuggled closer and before long clung to Josh, its claws digging into his side. This pain felt good, and Josh did nothing to avoid it.

Josh had nodded off when a bump in the road came to his dreams like a giant hand striking him.

He awoke in a cold sweat, breathing fast. The cub awoke also, tense, eyes dancing. Josh watched with fascination as the cub drew a front paw to its nose and sucked the pad, making a loud, rhythmic clucking, almost like humming.

The pickup slowed, turning onto gravel for the last mile home. As they pulled in the yard, the cub came to his feet, stiff legged and on guard. When they stopped, Pokey leaped frantically under the table and cowered. Josh crawled to his feet and stared out the window.

His mother, Libby, stood in the yard, eggs bunched in her apron. Rubber boots and baggy pants made her look fat, but she wasn't. Her waist-length hair was wrapped in a bun.

Caring for her hair was about the only thing she ever did for herself. Since Dad started drinking, she sat alone after chores, her callused fingers stroking the black river of hair, twisting it into tight braids.

"Sam, where is Josh?" she called, depositing her apron of eggs in the grass.

"In back," came Sam's muffled reply.

Josh grabbed the rope and opened the camper door. Libby met him. "What in tarnation?" she exclaimed, eyeing his tattered clothes and bruises. Then she spotted the cub.

Josh threw himself into her arms, sobbing.

"Josh, what's wrong?"

Before Sam appeared, Josh half-wept, half-whispered, "We killed his mom . . . we killed his mom." Then he dropped from her arms and dragged

Pokey toward the barn. The cub strained on the rope as a black-and-white border collie sprinted across the grass, barking.

"Mud Flap, stay away!" Josh screamed. The dumb dog had earned her name chasing trucks and biting at their mud flaps. Josh watched the dog stop. Her ears drooped, and her tail tucked down between her legs. Pokey and Mud Flap could get acquainted later.

Entering the barn, the cool, quiet air muffled his parents' talk. He coaxed the cub to an empty horse stall—the horses were out on summer pasture. As Josh removed the rope, Pokey spun and bit his hand, clamping like a vise grip. Josh jerked back but failed to pry the cub loose. Gasping, he grabbed his neck and bit into his buff-colored nose. Pokey let go with a loud squall, landing roughly on the stall floor.

"Pokey, quit it! Let's not hurt each other," Josh scolded as the cub ran to the far side of the high-sided box stall. Josh nursed his bruised hand as he went to get a pail of water. Next he threw in half a bale of straw for bedding. What should he feed the cub? Any more cookies would probably give Pokey a stomachache.

The barn door opened, and Josh turned to see his mother. Libby's quiet voice broke the cool air. "Josh, come here—let's look at you."

Josh approached, head bowed.

"What happened?" she asked, touching his swollen cheek.

Josh pulled away from her touch. "I got run over by a lawn mower," he said, forcing a weak smile.

His mother failed to smile and waited patiently in the shadowy light. There was no escaping her question. Reluctantly Josh pointed at his ragged pants and scraped leg. "That . . . got that by falling on some shale." Next he pointed to the bruises, cuts, and dried spots of blood on his arms and shoulder. "Got these when I caught the cub."

"What happened there?" Libby asked, pointing to his bleeding hand.

"Pokey bit me."

"Pokey?"

"Yeah, that's what I called him."

"Is your hand okay?"

Josh nodded. "I bit him back."

Libby shook her head. "How about your cut lip and swollen cheek?" she asked.

"It's nothing, Mom."

"What happened?" Libby's voice sounded gentle but stern.

"I can't tell you," Josh said, whispering. He knew if his dad ever asked him a question, he had to answer. But Mom was different. She knew sometimes people couldn't tell the truth without hurting someone. That didn't mean Josh could lie—it meant he kept his mouth shut.

For several minutes Libby waited, then walked over, putting her arms around his shoulders. "Okay, we'll talk about it later. Come on up to the house— let's get you patched up."

Josh looked up. "Mom, please, let me stay here. Pokey's lost his mom and is real scared. And he's hungry—all he's had to eat are your oatmeal cookies and some bread."

"So, my cookies are so bad you're feeding them to the bears, are you?" she said, rolling her lips in a smile.

Josh saw her eyes glint and he smiled back. "I ate a bunch, too, but Pokey was really hungry," he said. Quickly he lost his smile. "Mom, what can I feed him?"

"Why don't you call Otis," Libby said. "He might know."

Josh nodded. He hadn't thought of calling Otis. The old man was a friend of Josh's. Well, sort of— he took care of wild animals, and he let Josh help him. Otis was kind of weird, but still Josh liked him.

Libby set her hand on Josh's shoulder. "Josh, are you sure your father killed Pokey's mom?"

Again Josh nodded. "I saw Pokey run after Dad shot and I found him sleeping near the gut pile."

Libby looked up thoughtfully. "Listen, why don't you call Otis from the barn phone. I'll go up to the house and get stuff to fix you up. Be back in a jiffy."

"Mom," Josh called as she left.

She turned. "What is it, Josh?"

Josh hesitated. "Thanks."

Libby smiled as she turned. "We've got to take care of Pokey," she called over her shoulder. "Now, go call Otis."

CHAPTER 5

GENTLY, Otis Sinclair resplinted the mangled wing of a great horned owl. "Easy, girl," he hummed bitterly. "A teeny old bullet can't whup us."

The proud raptor struggled to stand, but too much life had seeped from its gunshot wound. Otis gripped the big owl, avoiding its needle-sharp talons. Carefully he pried open its beak and poked in chunks of meat. Many more weeks of mothering might save the owl, but he doubted it would ever fly again. And all because of a whim, a prank, someone's foolishness.

"Can't people see what they're doing?" Otis asked aloud, resting the owl gently in its chicken-wire enclosure. "They kill you, girl, and they're killing themselves—we don't have a dozen worlds to practice on."

Otis stroked his long silver-splashed hair, his eyes watery with anger. It hadn't taken a bullet to waste his own life. He'd done that by teaching at the university and fighting for environmental issues—thinking someone cared. Simply put, spitting at the wind.

Otis remembered the final straw: the Fish and Game Department began issuing hunting permits on buffalo and grizzly bears. Was that why these animals had been saved from near extinction—to hunt them?

That day Otis resigned from the university, and from society. He bought a wooded lot away from town and surrounded the land with large orange keep-out signs.

Still a wildlife biologist at heart, he allowed the Fish and Game Department to bring in wounded animals for rehabilitation—as long as people stayed away. Rehabilitation was such a nice word. It evoked images of eagles soaring, once-crippled deer bounding through the forest, coyotes made well and yipping happily on moonlit hillsides. Actually Otis suspected the Fish and Game office considered this a form of disposal. Precious few animals ever found their way back to survival in the wild.

And those that did? Last year he spent months nursing a white-tail buck back from a gunshot wound. Two months after releasing it on a secluded hillside, he saw it pass through town thrown across the hood of a hunter's truck. Why did he even bother? Maybe this was how he fought back, one animal at a time: one duck, one deer, one owl, one raccoon, one pigeon, one coyote, one skunk.

The telephone's ring interrupted his gloomy thoughts. He ignored it, cooing softly to the big owl. Even wounded, the bird rested with composed dignity.

"A chunk of dirt has more feelings than the low-life who shot you, girl," Otis said, irked by the continued ringing of the phone. With a grumble he ambled toward the annoyance—whomever it was knew he was here. "What?" he answered, growling to strike the intruder with his gravelly voice.

After a moment's silence he heard young Josh McGuire's voice. "Hello . . . Otis?"

"No, he's out back ordering a new world from the Sears catalog. Can I give him a message?"

"Otis, this is Josh."

"I know that," Otis said, reluctantly pulling the thick edge from his voice. "Haven't you anything better to do?"

"Otis, can you tell me something?" the shy voice queried.

"Sure, I can tell anybody anything. Never does any good though. Nobody's listening." A silence on the phone dulled Otis's sarcasm. "Yeah, son, what do you want?" he asked.

"Ah . . . what would you feed a bear cub?"

"Don't tell me you've got a cub?"

"I didn't say that," Josh stammered. "Just curious."

Otis scratched his chin. His young friend never asked anything without good reason—and he liked that. Josh had first trespassed up his driveway several years earlier, asking to mow the lawn. Otis tried to scare him off with a snarly remark about wanting to let the grass grow. But when Josh caught sight of the animals, he dashed back among the pens.

All the threats and cussing in the world couldn't chase the youngster away from the animals. In the end, Otis let him stay. Now Josh came by every week to help feed.

Otis cleared his throat. "Well, Josh . . . I suppose I'd, ah, let me think. Is it hurt?"

Josh's voice sounded short. "No! And I didn't even say there was a cub. I just wanted to know what you'd feed one."

"Okay, okay! Listen . . . young cubs follow their mothers around and get their noses into everything. They chew on spring grass and dig for grubs, but mostly they nurse."

"He can't do that. I . . . I mean, what if the mother isn't there?" Desperation keened Josh's voice.

Otis gripped the phone. "Josh, first find a baby bottle and cut a bigger slit in the nipple. Give him lots of protein, like lamb mix, eggs, and some oatmeal."

"Otis, you think he'll suck from a bottle?"

"It should. Cubs are like lambs—they'll suck anything. I've seen cubs suck on each other's ears. By the way, how old a cub are we talking about?"

Josh paused. "Real young."

"Well, this year's cubs would be about sixteen weeks old—not much bigger than a small dog."

"He's bigger than . . . I mean, he would be a little bit bigger than that, wouldn't he?"

Otis coughed. "Could be. Now, Josh, you tell me why—"

"Thanks, Otis," Josh interrupted, hanging up with a click.

Otis rubbed his chin. The youngster was his *friend*, although he hated employing that term with any human. Maybe it was because Josh enjoyed animals. Whatever the reason, Otis had made the boy the single exception to his boycott of humanity. Whatever Josh was up to, it worried Otis.

Josh wanted to tell Otis about the cub, but he couldn't, not without tattling on Dad—then Dad would really get mad. Sam hated Otis and said the hermit was a bad influence. It seemed to have something to do with hunting. The more Josh got to liking Otis's animals, the less he liked to go hunting. After Dad started drinking, Josh grew to truly hate hunting. Dad blamed this all on Otis.

Once Josh had asked Otis if he ever hunted. The answer surprised Josh. "A long time ago I did," Otis said. "It was kinda fun, sneaking around and trying to outfox critters. But then I got to helping a friend save a hurt eagle. I learned that animals had feelings too, and helping a critter live was more fun than making it die." Looking down now at the cub sleeping curled in the straw, Josh had to agree with Otis.

In the barn Josh found a big feeding bottle—the kind used for starting calves. Next he rummaged through the kitchen until he had a bowl of food mixed up. When he offered the cub the first batch, it stood on its hind legs and gripped the big bottle, sucking and gulping. Josh drew the cub to his side as it drank, its black ball-bearing eyes peering off into space.

That night Josh slept in the barn. He rolled out his sleeping bag in the straw and let the cub crawl in and snuggle. After sucking its pads and humming, the cub wrapped both front paws around Josh—all night squirming closer.

At daybreak Josh awoke to his father's footsteps. He glanced up to find Sam staring into the box stall. The cub slept soundly.

"Josh," Sam said hoarsely. "I called the game warden and told him about the cub."

"Did you tell him we shot its mother?"

Sam kicked the stall door, waking up the cub. He started to say something loudly and then bit his words. "I told him we found it abandoned."

Josh cringed and eyed his father. "Can we keep him?"

"No, the warden will be by tomorrow. I'll stick around and hand over the cub after you've left for school."

"He can't have Pokey."

"I'm afraid it's not your choice. Go ahead and play, but don't get too attached 'cause the cub's not yours."

"It's not theirs either," Josh mumbled, staring down. The cub was on its feet, stretching. It yawned, extending a long curled tongue.

Sam turned and left the barn.

Josh panicked. What would happen to the cub— was there anybody he could ask? Again he called Otis and let the phone ring forever. When Otis finally answered, Josh held the phone out away from his ear.

"What?" Otis shouted.

Otis's gruff shouting didn't bother Josh—not like when his dad shouted. In fact, it was kind of funny. "Otis, it's me again." He shuffled his feet in the straw.

"What are you feeding now—an elephant?"

"Otis, what would the game warden do with a cub if its mother was dead?"

"Probably give it to the state research lab."

"What do they do with 'em?"

"Disease studies mostly, testing different drugs and vaccines. Josh, I want to know, why all these questions?"

"Otis, do the tests hurt 'em?"

"Well . . . yes and no. Most end up dying."

"You mean it kills 'em?" Josh exclaimed.

"That's right. Now, you tell me why you're asking!"

"Otis, what if I . . . I mean, if someone let the cub go?"

"Don't do that! Coyotes, eagles, big owls, mountain lions, even male bears would kill it. It needs the mother for protection. They are—"

Josh interrupted, "Why do they hunt bears then, if the mothers can get killed?"

"Because most people don't care."

Josh felt desperate. "How can they not care?" he asked.

"It gets easy after a while," Otis said.

"Otis, would they let you raise a cub?"

"Not unless it was wounded, and then only until it was well enough for research. Now! Before I say another word, you have some explaining. What's all this about?"

"I'll tell you later, Otis—I promise. Good-bye."

Otis started to protest, but Josh hung up and returned to the stall. He stared at Pokey. Tomorrow the game warden was coming—nothing could change that. He knelt beside the cub, which looked up with sparkling, innocent eyes.

"Pokey, you're going to die—and there's nothing I can do!" Josh said sadly, tossing up a clump of straw. Pokey pounced on it, then turned his nose for more. Josh tossed another handful up. The cub leaped, but the straw separated and drifted down, settling like gold dust on the cub's black woolly hair. Soon Pokey pounced on Josh, biting and shaking his pant leg. With a playful grunt he wiggled his fat rump.

For nearly an hour they played in the straw, with Josh wrestling and tumbling and laughing. Finally the cub yawned wide and crawled onto Josh's lap and began clucking against its paw. They nestled close.

"Pokey, are you afraid of dying?" Josh asked quietly, becoming serious.

The cub tilted his head and looked up quizzically.

"You don't understand, do you?" Josh said, trembling. Then he sobbed, terrified by his next thought. He blurted it out. "Even if Dad kills me, I won't let them take you," he said, his voice cracking. "We'll run away."

CHAPTER 6
CHAPTER

THE PLAN came to Josh bit by bit. Running away scared him silly—but so did the idea of Pokey dying. The barn door creaked, and he jumped.

His father entered. "Josh," he said, "We've been invited to Gilbert's for supper. If you want to go, you'll need to get changed."

"You mean I can stay with Pokey if I want?"

Sam's voice tensed. "Mother said it's up to you. I think it's high time you forgot this foolishness."

"It's not that I don't want to go, it's just . . . well, Pokey is lonely."

"Lonely! Bahh!" His father spit and glared down, his cheeks and forehead twitching. "You forget that damn bear, you hear. You're making something out of nothing."

"They'll kill him, Dad!"

"You killed him when you brought him off the mountain. Get that through your stump of a head, Son. Now go get ready. We're leaving in a half hour."

"I'm staying here."

Sam spun, fists tight and eyes burning.

Josh ran over against the edge of the stall. "Don't hurt me, Dad. Please."

The sound of Libby calling chickens in the farmyard made Sam pause. "Don't you ever tell me what to do!" he snapped, stomping out the door.

Josh breathed fast. Was Dad right? Had he taken the cub from its mom? Remembering, he shook his head. No! They had orphaned the cub, and now it would die. Josh walked over and sat beside the cub. Why did his dad say things like that? He wasn't drunk right now, but he spoke like he was. Is that what drinking did to a person—it made you lie? None of this would have happened if Tye hadn't died.

No matter what, Josh couldn't let Pokey die. When his parents left, he would take the cub and run away to the mountains. But, no, that wouldn't work. Mom and Dad would only be gone a few hours—not enough time to run very far. Memory of getting hit by his father hung like a black cloud over every thought. Whatever he did, he had to save Pokey.

Josh brainstormed. The Bridger Mountains north of home were the closest, but also the first place they would look. He'd never been to the Spanish Peaks southwest of Bozeman, or the Crazies to the east. He knew the remote and rugged Tom Miner Basin well, north of Yellowstone Park. But it was seventy impossible miles away.

Thoughts scrambling, he watched his parents pull out of the drive. He'd get ready now, then leave after his parents went to bed tonight. That way he'd have all night to get away.

Quickly he heaped into his backpack a box of dried milk, two dozen eggs cracked into a gallon jug, some oatmeal, a can of soup, pancake mix, his jackknife and canteen. He scooped three candy bars from the refrigerator along with some jerky and bread. Then he stopped. What was he doing? How could he carry this much stuff? He could leave the canteen empty— most places had streams. But even still, the pack weighed a ton. Where did he plan to go? He couldn't hitchhike at night, and surely not with a cub. Josh looked down. His legs were shaking.

Still he kept getting ready. He laid out his jacket and ran to the toolshed for fishing line. There an idea struck him. Parked at one end, under a dusty tarp, sat Tye's old Enduro 125 motocross cycle. After Tye's death, Dad had stored the cycle away, refusing to sell it. Now riding it seemed unthinkable. Not so much because of Josh's age—Tye had let him ride it often enough. Shoot, Josh had driven tractor since he was nine. He'd even driven combine. No, it was something else: the cycle belonged to the dead.

Tye wouldn't mind—he'd have wanted to save the cub. Josh thought of something else: was it wrong to ride without a license—probably? But it was wrong to kill Pokey's mother, too. And it would be wrong to kill Pokey. Shoot, lots of things were wrong! Gritting his teeth, Josh filled the Honda with gas and checked the oil.

After resting the heavy machine outside the toolshed on its kickstand, Josh turned the key and pulled out the choke. Again and again he jumped on the kick starter. No luck. He tinkered with the choke and tried again. Still nothing. Deliberately he leaped up and down until his leg burned and sweaty hair mopped his forehead. He'd almost given up when the engine sputtered and caught. Stinky smoke belched out, and a tinny whine broke the quiet air. Josh raced the engine, then quickly shut it off.

To carry Pokey, he fashioned a wooden cover on a plastic milk crate. This, along with a small can of gas, he mounted to the cycle rack with bungee cords. Everything was ready. He returned the cycle to the shed and hid it under the tarp. His backpack bulged beneath his sleeping bag—the load would be heavy even on the cycle. After shoving the pack under the tarp, he went to the barn to wait. Time dragged slowly, and Josh agonized. Had he forgotten anything?

When his parents returned, they stopped by the barn. "You have school in the morning," Sam said. "Let's go up to the house."

"Can I sleep with Pokey again?" Josh pleaded.

Sam started to protest, but Libby interrupted. "Yes," she said. Her hardened tone and sullen look caused Sam to grumble. He mumbled something as he followed her from the barn.

When they had left, Josh guessed it to be nearly nine-thirty. The last rays of sun had softened the air. Josh stared out at the clouds through an old dirt-glazed window. Tinted, billowy mounds piled up on the horizon like heaps of red cotton dumped at the edge of the world.

Before going to bed, his mother brought down a small snack and an extra blanket. "You've grown fond of that little guy, haven't you?" she asked.

Josh nodded.

"Josh . . ." His mother struggled with her words. "Don't get too attached. It'll only hurt worse."

Josh's voice shook. "What about Pokey? He'll die. That's what Otis said—he'll die. Bears hurt too, Mom."

Libby paused. "I've tried talking to your father . . . it doesn't help."

"Dad won't even admit he killed Pokey's mom."

"Are you sure it was his mom?" she asked.

"Like I told you, Pokey was sleeping near the gut pile, and I know I saw him run away after Dad shot.' Josh paused, embarrassed. "Mom, white stuff even came out of the dead bear's tits. Doesn't that mean she had a cub?"

Libby examined Josh oddly. "Josh," she said, "I think I know what happened to your cheek yesterday. This last—"

"Mom, it wasn't—"

"Just listen to me! This last year has been hard. I'm not making excuses for your father, but he's a good man. I'm so scared for him . . . and for us. Just remember, whatever happens, I love you. Okay?"

Josh nodded.

After Libby left, Josh called Mud Flap into the barn. He didn't want her barking. Impatiently he watched the house, wishing he could be in bed like everyone else. Why couldn't it be like it used to be with Dad hugging him good-night and bidding him to go sleep with the angels? Tonight his father seemed a million miles away, and Josh's journey would surely not take him to visit any angels.

Finally the last house light blinked off. He'd wait a bit longer so his parents could fall asleep—but not too long. Soon the moon would be up and make his getaway visible.

He poked a scribbled note over a nail on the stall door. It said he wouldn't come home until he could keep Pokey and until the warden quit letting people hunt bears. Boy, would this make Dad spit nails!

After feeding the cub, Josh filled the bottle and tucked it upright in the pack—Pokey might need to eat on the run. Next he borrowed Mud Flap's collar and wrestled it on the cub. Pokey thought it was a game until he tried to remove the tight strap. Then he tugged and clawed at it with his front paws. Quickly Josh attached the rope and took a deep breath. Everything was ready. Moving slowly, he slipped into the night. The cub hesitated but followed. So did Mud Flap.

"Mud Flap, go lie down—stay!" Josh whispered loudly.

Mud Flap cowered into the darkness.

Once inside the dark toolshed, Josh fumbled the cover off the cycle, then lifted the cub grunting and struggling into the milk crate. A chunk of candy bar quieted the protest. Josh held his breath and looked out at the darkened house. Before shouldering his pack, he propped some chunks of lumber under the tarp. Dad might not notice the Honda missing—if he did, boy would he go nuts. Josh tried not to think of his father as he pulled on Tye's helmet. The helmet wobbled loosely but made him feel more grown up.

Gravel crunched under the knobby wheels as Josh pushed the cycle out of the shed and across the yard. An upstairs light blinked back on in the house. Josh's heart raced, and he pushed the cycle to his right, crowding the edge of the driveway. Soon another light came on downstairs. It was getting hard to swallow. If they turned on the yard light, he'd be a sitting duck. But he couldn't drop the cycle—Pokey would bawl.

His mother's silhouette appeared as she closed the kitchen windows. Soon the downstairs light went off, followed shortly by the upstairs light. Again the house stood dark. Josh sighed and pushed as fast as he could out the drive. Crickets chorused around him, becoming silent as he passed, then renewing their pulsing rhythm.

The pack grew heavy. Half-a-dozen times Josh stopped, resting the burden on the seat. His arms ached, and his legs burned. He fought the urge to get on and ride—the air was too quiet. Sweat soaked his forehead, and his tongue stuck like a big wad of cotton in his mouth. Finally, after nearly a mile, Josh saw the highway. He dropped the pack to the ground.

Fighting to catch his breath, he crawled on and turned the key. He kicked hard. Silence. Again and again he kicked, a knot forming in his stomach. What if the motor wouldn't start?

"C'mon," he whispered, leaping high and kicking again.

A deafening roar swallowed the still night, and Josh cringed, glancing over his shoulder. Pokey bumped from side to side, grunting and clawing at the crate.

"Easy, fellow, it won't hurt you," Josh said loudly.

The engine drowned out his voice as he pulled on his pack. With the headlight off, he drove to the highway in second gear. There he stopped. When he snapped on the headlight and turned to check on Pokey, he heard a noise. Out of the darkness came Mud Flap, panting heavily.

CHAPTER 7
CHAPTER

JOSH GASPED. "Mud Flap! No! You can't follow!"

The winded border collie gazed up, her head cocked.

Josh threw a rock. Not meaning to, he actually hit her, but she remained, whining.

"Get! Go home. I'm tryin' to run away, you dumb dog!"

The dog watched silently.

"Dang you, Mud Flap, you're wreck'n my plans."

Why hadn't he left her in the barn? Now there wasn't time to take her back. Even if he did, she might start barking. He couldn't just leave her—she would keep following until she got lost.

Mud Flap ran forward and jumped her front paws up.

"I know what you want. You think you can ride on the gas tank like you did with Tye," Josh grumbled.

The small dog yipped and tilted her head, ears perked.

"I'm not Tye and you're not going with—I'm runnin' away!"

Mud Flap barked again, jumping deftly up onto the gas tank. Before Josh could push her off, she wrapped her paws over the handlebars, pushing her hind legs stiffly against the seat. She faced forward as if the whole matter were settled.

Josh swatted Mud Flap's rump. "Get off!"

Mud Flap stared straight ahead, not twitching a hair.

Josh eyed the dog. Stupid mutt! What could he do? Nothing, he admitted. Reluctantly he eased the clutch out, heading into the night. Mud Flap perched, rigid, like a hood ornament, the wind flapping her ears. "I hope you like running away!" Josh shouted.

Overhead the sky hung like a black bowl shot full of bright BB holes. Josh couldn't see Pokey, but the cycle swerved whenever the cub moved. He rode on. Near Bozeman he stopped and adjusted the pack straps biting into his shoulders. To avoid town, he'd have to risk taking the interstate. Farther east he could get off onto frontage road.

Nervously he pulled onto the interstate. For five miles he saw no cars. Then, nearer Bozeman Pass, lights started gaining on him. He sped up, but they overtook him. A huge semitruck roared past, buffeting the helmet down over Josh's eyes. Mud Flap started to jump, but Josh grabbed her with one hand. The cycle bounced and swerved as Pokey panicked. Desperately Josh clutched Mud Flap and the handlebar, tilting his head back to peer out from under the helmet.

As the truck roared off into the night, Josh slowed.

"You're going to get us hurt, you bonehead!" he screamed at Mud Flap. "You should have stayed home, you dumb stupid dog!"

The small dog trembled.

"I should have, too," Josh added with a mumble, finally steering the cycle down the Jackson Creek exit and onto frontage road. The night grew colder as he continued east, then south through Paradise Valley.

Suddenly a parked police car flashed by in the night. Josh stiffened and sat tall, his heart pounding against his jacket. Did he look thirteen? Maybe he should pull over and try to explain, or say he was sorry. Instead he kept going. It was hard to tell if the police car had followed, and for several miles Josh imagined lights chasing him.

Topping a small rise, Josh slowed and looked back at the ranch lights sprinkling the valley. Vibration had numbed his arms and legs—even his guilt. He squinted his dry, sore eyes at the road stripes flickering past him out of the night. Steep canyon shadows loomed by, signaling the end of Paradise Valley. Josh shivered. How long had he been riding?

Finally he saw the turnoff to Tom Miner Basin. Now the going would be rutted and across muddy gravel. He gripped the handlebars harder and kept going. When the highway was safely behind him, Josh stopped to add the extra gas.

Mud Flap bounded to the ground, and Josh struggled to crawl off. His whole body was cold and sore. He stomped his feet and swung his arms. Awkwardly he emptied the gas can into the tank and crawled back on—he had to stay moving. Mud Flap jumped back up as the engine roared to life. The cub squalled and bit at the sides of the crate.

As he rode, Josh thought of new problems. He had food for Pokey, but not for Mud Flap. If Mom and Dad did agree to his note, how would they contact him? And if they didn't, then what?

He'd forgotten his brown sweater, a flashlight, and extra matches—he had only one small bookful. As bad as he was at lighting fires, he might use them all up on the first try. He did have along the eighty-seven dollars he'd saved for his new bike. But what good would money be up on Ram's Horn Peak—not many hamburger stands up there.

Each thought made Josh more lonely. Running away was sure hard. Above, the moon hung like a white-hot ember, looking lonely. Suddenly tears blurred the road. "Doggone wind," Josh muttered. This whole thing was stupid. Real stupid.

Ahead, a narrow gravel road jutted to the right. Josh slowed. That went up Rock Creek. Otis had mentioned this road, little more than a rutted jeep path. It wrapped around the back side of Ram's Horn Peak and joined a trail leading to a meadow below the peak. Farther around the mountain was a small lake.

Rock Creek climbed much higher before hitting trailhead than did the Tom Miner road. There were also fewer people. He might even be able to ride the trail. The catch: it was twice as far, the road was rougher, and he might get lost. Josh stopped and let his mind argue the issue. Finally, pressing his lips tight, he pulled right onto the thin trenched lane.

The going was slow, bobbing and weaving along. Potholes bounced Mud Flap off twice. When Josh reached the trail, a knot bit at his stomach. Ahead, moonlight soaked the path, exposing sharp cliffs and deep ravines on each side. Did he dare ride? At night? The thought of hiking with the straps digging into his raw shoulders made up his mind. He shoved Mud Flap off—from here on she could keep up. "Here we go, Pokey," Josh shouted, gunning the engine. The cub hunkered down, eyes glinting wildly in the moonlight.

The cycle twisted and jarred up the trail. Josh gripped hard as the narrow path climbed a steep slope. He held his breath and revved the engine, roaring over the hill, tires slipping and spinning. Mud Flap ran behind, panting. The headlight beam skipped around on the hillside. Josh wanted to stop, but a warm anger came over him. If he stopped, Pokey would die. "No one's going to kill you, Pokey. No one," Josh yelled back, cranking harder on the throttle.

The mountain became a nightmare of curves and bumps. When at last he reached the meadow below the peaks, his arms were weak and heavy. He couldn't keep a grip on the cycle, and it heeled over in the grass as he got off. Sputtering, it stopped. Mud Flap jumped out of the way, but Pokey's crate smacked the ground. The empty gas can jarred loose with a loud clank.

The cub bumped about frantically inside the crate, clawing at the sides. Josh scrambled to his feet and unhooked the crate, righting it on the ground. Pokey had to settle down before getting out.

It took a minute to catch his breath, then Josh lifted the cycle upright. That done, he collapsed in the grass. The crisp mountain air had a sharp bite he hadn't noticed on the trail. Ram's Horn Peak loomed in the moonlight and cast a deep shadow far across the meadow. The night seemed deadly quiet without the screaming cycle.

As Pokey settled down, Josh pressed pieces of chocolate bar inside the crate. It would take a while to gain back the friendship bounced and jolted out of the cub over the last several hours. Reluctantly Pokey started nibbling. Josh yawned and struggled to keep his eyes open. It had to be near dawn judging by how low the moon hung. Staying awake all night was getting to be a habit.

He crumbled up the last of the candy bar and scattered it in the crate, then eased open the top. The cub shoveled its nose around while Josh gently tied the rope to its collar. Barely had the knot been pulled tight when Pokey spun and bit hard into Josh's wrist.

"Ouch!" Josh screamed, yanking away.

The cub held on, clawing and shaking Josh's wrist with a steel grip. Josh grunted sharply as a black-and-white bundle streaked out of the dark. Mud Flap sank her teeth into Pokey's shoulder and pummeled the cub with a throaty growl. The cub let loose in surprise as Mud Flap intensified her attack, snapping and biting. The night blurred with teeth and growls and twisting bodies rolling through the grass.

"Mud Flap, no! I said no!"

The border collie spun free and stood growling, crouched for another attack. Pokey rubbed his nose, glaring at the dog and blowing sharply through his lips.

"Ah, dang, why did you bite me, Pokey? I'm tryin' to help you. Can't you see that?" Josh said, rubbing his sore wrist. He felt wetness. In the darkness he licked a finger and tasted blood. Mud Flap kept growling. "Okay, that's enough," Josh said. "You were good, Mud Flap. You were good, girl."

The dog wagged her tail slowly, keeping her eyes pinned on the cub. Josh led Pokey through the grass and tied him to a large, scrubby sagebrush. Then he went back for his pack and sleeping bag. In the morning he could hide the cycle. Now he was too tired and sore.

Josh spread his sleeping bag on the grass near Pokey. Gosh it was cold! Mud Flap snuggled close as the cub played, digging and climbing all over the brush. Before falling asleep, Josh noticed pale red streaks tinting the dark sky. He awoke once to hear Pokey's rhythmic cluck and to feel the fuzzy hair of the cub's paw around his neck.

As he fell back to sleep, a strong wind picked up, and a deep ominous rumble rolled across the meadow. The sound blended with his sleep—in his dreams he was struggling to ride a cycle up a trail that grew steeper and steeper.

CHAPTER 8
CHAPTER

SAM MCGUIRE jerked the note off the stall door and stared in disbelief.

> I can't let Pokey die so I'm running away.
> I'll come home when I can keep Pokey and
> when nobody can hunt bears anymore.
>
> Josh

Run away? The bum! The little scalawag! Sam slammed the stall door closed. School started in an hour. This time Josh had gotten too big for his britches. He had flat out disobeyed, and Sam would have none of it.

Maybe the cub did belong to the she-bear he'd shot. But so what? It hadn't happened on purpose. And you didn't just walk into the Fish and Game office and say, "Hello, I'm Sam McGuire. Could you please stop hunting bears because my son wants you to." Even if Josh could keep the cub, Sam was danged if he'd have a bear running around. He crumpled the note in his hand.

"Libby!" he hollered, stomping into the house. "Get your coat."

Libby met him, wiping her hands on her apron. The smell of bacon and muffins filled the air. "What's wrong?"

Sam tossed the wadded note at her. She picked it off the floor, slowly drawing her hand to her mouth. "Oh, poor Josh. I should have guessed this might happen."

Sam bunched his lips in anger. "When I find him, I'll—"

"Sam, he's only thirteen," she interrupted.

"I don't care if he's two."

Libby furrowed her brows with concern. "What are we going to do?" she asked.

"Go find him, that's what—he can't drag a cub too far. Get your coat. We'll drive the logging roads."

"Shouldn't we call the sheriff?"

"No!" Sam shot back as he left. "This is our problem."

Libby grabbed her jacket and ran after him, pulling off her apron. Soon Sam was driving the foothills as she rode along quietly. The June air had an unusual bite to it. Thick black clouds charred the western edge of a pewter sky.

After miles of searching, Sam hit his fist on the dash. "Where is that beggar?"

"Did you see Mud Flap back at the farm?" Libby asked.

"No, Josh probably took her, too. With his nerve, he probably took along a durned cow."

"Sam," Libby begged.

He ignored her. They had searched now for nearly three hours. He reached under the seat and pulled out an open fifth of whiskey. The sullen look he got from Libby irritated him. Josh got his mute tongue from her. She said more with her mouth shut than open.

Libby broke her thick silence. "Sam, let's go home and call the school. We need to call the sheriff, too."

"What can they do?" Sam spit. His knuckles were white from clenching the steering wheel.

"Help us look!"

"Yeah, and let the radio stations and newspapers know we've raised a knuckle-brained delinquent."

Libby's voice cracked and she dabbed her eyes. "I don't care, as long as we get Josh back. I just want . . ." Her voice trailed off.

Brooding, Sam spun the pickup around and headed for the ranch. The sky had grown darker. North and west, monstrous thunderclouds bunched, spitting jagged bolts of lightning at the horizon. A swig off an empty bottle angered Sam worse. He tossed the worthless container to the floor. It wasn't bad enough with Tye dead. Now Josh had run away, and his wife was crying her fool eyes out.

"Go ahead," he said, pulling the car in the yard. "Call anybody you want if it makes you feel better. Just leave me out of it." He stepped out and slammed the door.

Libby stammered over the phone, trying to explain Josh's disappearance. After a litany of seemingly pointless questions, the sheriff's office agreed to send out a deputy. Libby paced back and forth, waiting—

what else should she do? She needed to call the school. That done, she tried to concentrate. Who would Josh trust?—maybe Otis Sinclair. Quickly she dialed. After a dozen endless rings, she heard a click.

"What?" a sharp voice growled.

Libby nearly hung up. "Ah, Mr. Sinclair. I'm glad you're home. This is Josh's mother, Libby."

"Call me Otis," said the gruff voice. "Mr. Sinclair makes it sound like you're collecting money. I suppose the little scamp's got you making his phone calls now."

"Josh ran away," Libby blurted, rolling the telephone cord back and forth between her sweaty fingers. "I don't know why I'm calling, except Josh thinks the world of you."

"A darn hermit isn't much of a hero. Now, why would he run away?"

Libby hesitated and lowered her voice. "His father orphaned a cub, but denies it." She looked fearfully over her shoulder. "Josh found the cub sleeping near the mother's gut pile and brought it home—said he talked to you about it, and that you said it would die if he gave it up or let it go."

"He didn't tell me he had a cub, although I guessed as much. He asked a passel of questions that didn't make sense till now. So the cub is with him?"

"Yes, and he left this note." Libby read it.

"I can't help you," Otis said, his voice guarded. "In thirty years, I couldn't get the government to skip a coffee break—they sure won't change the law for some kid."

Libby fought to steady her voice. "I don't care about the law. I'm worried about Josh. Lately Sam's been awful hard on him. If Josh calls anyone, it might be you. Please let us know if he does. Sam doesn't think he'll get far. Figures he'll come home soon, tired and scared."

"Mrs. McGuire, don't underestimate your boy. You have quite a son . . . no thanks to his father."

Libby swallowed and bit her words. "Otis, it wasn't always this way. Deep down, Sam's a good man."

"Yeah," Otis said, "and deep down you get to China. Take my word. If Josh ran away, he did it right."

"What do you mean by that?"

"Just don't look to find him too easy. He's got more spunk than a den of badgers. Did you call the sheriff's department?"

"Yeah, they're sending an officer. Otis, I'm so scared."

"And right you should be. They'd better hustle. This storm that's brewing, I've never seen anything like it."

"You think it's going to be bad?" Libby knew her voice shook with desperation.

"I do. The temperature's dropped thirty degrees in the last couple of hours, and it's still lightning. You ever seen lightning when it's cold enough for snow?"

"No, guess not," she said.

"Hope he's not caught out in the open. It might be a bigger bite than he can chew."

Libby scrambled for hope—some fragment she

could cling to and hug to her heart. But she found none. When Libby hung up she felt lost, and utter despair gnawed at her. Life was like dominoes—one day everything was so neat, then it caved in a piece at a time. First Tye's death, then Sam's drinking, now Josh—what if she lost him? She breathed deep, concentrating. She had to hang on. If she didn't? No! She couldn't think like that.

The screen door slammed. "You done calling all the neighbors?" Sam said, entering the house.

"I called the sheriff's department, the school, and . . . and Otis Sinclair."

Sam spun. "Why'd you call him? He's probably the one that put Josh up to this."

Libby didn't answer. She knew Sam had hated Otis from the first day Josh came home talking big about the animal man he'd met.

Sam raised his voice. "The Fish and Game was picking up the cub today. Did you call and tell them your knucklehead son ran away with it?"

"I'll call them," Libby said, picking up the phone. "He's your son, too," she added.

Sam gave her a harsh look, then stormed around the house slapping the wall and cussing vehemently.

Libby watched silently. What was happening? In the past, they'd always had each other. The bigger the debt or problem, the more pastures they had walked, hand in hand. Always he'd been there with a kind word or an encouraging smile. But no longer!

CHAPTER 9

CHAPTER

DEPUTY BREWSTER BINGHAM rested in his patrol car near the Bridger foothills. He nursed a cup of lukewarm coffee from his thermos and gazed up at the lush slopes splashed with buttercups, wild roses, and Indian paintbrush. June rains made them vivid against the verdant grasses. Beyond, rain clouds rolled upward on the horizon like dirty snowbanks.

Brewster adjusted his big body to relieve his sore leg. Out here away from town he could try to forget the night ten years ago when he took a bullet in the leg. But the pain always reminded him. He pinched his eyes closed and grimaced.

He rolled the window down to cool his face. A warbler's song floated in, clear and pure as a mountain lake. With it came the pungent smell of sage and an unexpected clap of thunder. Brewster glanced westward at the huge, black thunderheads churning and boiling in. The air held a curious chill and a menacing pall.

The radio squawked, "All units. Have report of a runaway child in the Bridger foothill area. Copy?"

Brewster started from his daze and reached dutifully for his microphone. "Roger, Dispatch. This is unit Twenty-Two."

"Twenty-Two, what's your location?"

"Off Highway Ten on Springhill."

"Twenty-Two, proceed to rural fire number two sixty-five, McGuire residence—three miles north of you and west on county road six. Do you copy?"

"Roger, Dispatch. Any details?"

"Negative, Twenty-Two. But forecast is calling for severe storms and blizzarding."

"Thank you, Dispatch. Twenty-Two out."

"Ten-four."

Blizzarding in June? A runaway boy? These were fearful things. Traffic violations, accidents, even robberies were pretty straightforward, the details concrete and usually forthcoming Runaways were different, their motives less clear. Children did things for reasons their parents often hated to admit.

As a deputy, Brewster headed up the Gallatin County Search and Rescue Department. This had taught him much about human nature. If someone was on the run, you had to know what they were running from. People who ran from themselves behaved differently from those who ran from the law. A person escaping responsibility acted different from someone filled with anger or revenge. The possibilities played out in Brewster's mind as he drove. The crack and peal of thunder broke into his thoughts. He eyed the sky. This was not going to be an ordinary storm.

As he pulled in the drive, a short, stout lady ran

toward him, her baggy pants flopping around her ankles. She had coal black hair tucked in a bun, and she clutched something in her left hand. Drawing closer, Brewster saw fear in her watery almond eyes. Proud, raw-boned cheeks pocketed her gaze.

A tall, thin man stood loose jointed in the doorway. His hard, chiseled look was all too familiar to Brewster, who had grown up on a ranch in southern Texas. He knew the adversity that hollowed out cheeks and carved such deep furrows in a forehead. Stepping from his car, Brewster saw no movement from the lanky man. A silent challenge had been issued.

"Howdy. Is this the McGuires?" he asked the lady.

"Yes, Officer," she breathed heavily. "I'm Libby McGuire. Can you help us find our son? I'm so afraid for—"

"Easy now. I reckon as we can help you, but first things first. I'm Deputy Bingham. When did you find your boy gone?"

"This morning when we went to get him up for school."

"He wasn't in his room?"

"He'd been sleeping in the barn with the cub."

"The cub—a bear cub?"

Libby nodded. "He ran away with it and our dog, Mud Flap."

"Where did this bear cub come from?"

Libby bit at her bottom lip and glanced fearfully over her shoulder. "Can you just find our son, Officer?"

Brewster saw the husband still leaning sullenly in

the doorway, a smirk on his face. There was more to this story than a runaway boy. "Can you get me a picture of your son?" he asked.

She nodded.

As she rushed off, Brewster turned toward Libby's husband. "Mr. McGuire," he called, "I've got a few questions."

The man lurched upright and sauntered over. "My name's Sam. What's there to ask? Our boy ran away."

Brewster smelled whiskey on the man and saw distrust and anger burning in his stare. He noted the time of day. Drinking could be a big part of any puzzle. "Mr. McGuire," he said, "I'm Deputy Bingham. How old is your boy?"

Sam scratched his head. "Thirteen, I think."

Libby returned, but Brewster kept his gaze leveled at Sam. "Where did he get the cub, and why did he run away with it?"

Sam gnawed on a straw stub, tension tugging at his lips. "He just found it and ran away because he's bullheaded."

"Just like that?" Brewster asked.

"Yeah. Just like that," Sam spit.

Brewster turned to Libby. "Is that right, Mrs. McGuire?"

Sam spun and faced Brewster squarely. "I told you what happened. Are you doubting me?"

Brewster never flinched. "Mr. McGuire," he drawled, "everybody sees things different."

Sam clenched his fists. "You think I'm lying?" he said.

Brewster paused a moment, measuring his man. "I think you have a boy that needs finding, and there's a storm cooking." He shifted his gaze back to Libby. "Now, Mrs. McGuire, is that how it all happened?" The look of fear in Libby's eyes told Brewster he had crowded too close.

Libby fidgeted. "Josh claimed Sam orphaned the cub up hunting," she said. "He said he saw the cub run when Sam shot. Then he found the cub sleeping near the gut pile."

Brewster turned to Sam. "Did you orphan the cub?"

Sam shook his head. "Josh is a little thief and a liar."

Brewster turned back. "That still doesn't explain why Josh ran away, Mrs. McGuire."

"The Fish and Game wouldn't let him keep the cub and would have sent it for research. So he left with the cub and our dog, Mud Flap. Here." Libby handed over Josh's picture and note.

Brewster read the boy's note before speaking. "I'll be honest with you," he said. "If he's gone to the mountains, this storm could spell real trouble. Is there anywhere else he might have gone?"

"Yeah," Sam said. "Otis Sinclair's. He probably gave Josh the idea to begin with."

"Who's Otis Sinclair?"

Libby spoke. "He's a friend that lives near here. Josh isn't there. I already called."

"He's no friend," Sam said. "He's a damn hermit, and I don't trust him."

"All right, I'll talk to him," Brewster said, a gust of cold wind stealing the last of his words. "If Josh is in the hills, the Search and Rescue crews won't be able to do much till the storm's over. I'll notify them, though, and get things ready. Contact your neighbors and see if anyone's seen him. I'll take this picture and get a dispatch to the media. We might get some leads."

Sam tugged at his pockets roughly, his eyes blazing. Then he stepped forward. "Listen, I don't want every gopher and coyote knowing our business. Let's forget this whole thing. I'll keep looking myself."

Libby trembled when she spoke. "Honey, please. It might help us find Josh."

"I said no! Thank you, Officer. We've wasted enough of your time."

Suddenly Libby turned on Sam. "Damn you, Sam! When Tye died, it wasn't your fault. But you've blamed yourself ever since. Josh ran away because he was afraid of you. If anything happens, God help you . . . it will be your fault, and I'll never forgive you."

"Get in the house," Sam ordered.

"Or you'll hit me like you did Josh," she said, taunting.

Brewster saw a flicker of surprise in Sam's angry eyes. This whole puzzle had a mess of pieces, and some were coming together.

"I said, get in the house!" Sam bellowed.

"Mrs. McGuire, you're welcome to ride to the station with me," Brewster offered.

"She's staying here," Sam said.

Brewster ignored Sam. "Would you like a ride?"

Libby drew in a deep breath and calmly dusted her hand across her jeans. "I appreciate your offer, Officer Bingham, but my place is here." She turned to Sam. "I'm staying—not because you ordered me to, but because this is my house, too. Officer, please get whatever help you can . . . and would you be so kind as to call me in an hour and see if I'm okay?"

Brewster riveted his gaze on Sam as he spoke. "I'd be happy to, Mrs. McGuire. In fact, I'm sure it will be necessary for me to call quite often as we need more information. Good day, Mrs. McGuire . . . Mr. McGuire." He nodded his chin at Sam, then turned calmly and paced himself back to the patrol car.

CHAPTER CHAPTER 10

JOSH AWOKE shivering. Was this a crazy dream? He saw trees, rocks, a stream, and a meadow blanketed in snow! He struggled to his feet, clawing at the nightmare. This place, where was he? The piercing wind and driving snow were real.

Then he remembered running away and the long lonely ride through the night. He'd fallen asleep in this meadow below Ram's Horn Peak. But the storm? Squinting into the wind, he saw Mud Flap and Pokey huddled together on the sleeping bag, staring up innocently. "Let's get outta here," Josh shouted.

He studied the cycle perched on its kickstand. Would anyone spot it? A sudden gust nearly twisted him off his feet—no fool would see it in this weather. He roused the animals from the bag and bundled it with his numb fingers. Why hadn't he brought gloves? Gripping Pokey's leash, he stuffed the bulky bedroll under one arm and swung his pack up.

"Come on! We've got to move!" Josh screamed with urgency as he scrambled and slipped toward the trees. The wind came like a wall of air, shoving and buffeting each step. First it whipped from the front, bending him over. Then from behind, sending Pokey bounding out ahead. Josh's ears and hands were bare to the raw wind. He buried his fists in his jacket pockets and tilted his head.

Why was this happening? Josh had never seen a storm like this. Not even in winter. This blizzard was wicked and evil. It was trying to hurt someone. Josh's thoughts muddled, and he fixed his gaze on the tree line. A gust drove him sideways, pelting his face with a spray of ice. Josh gasped. "Quit it!" he screamed desperately.

At last he crouched behind a lone rock to catch his breath and look back. The cub huddled against his legs. But where was Mud Flap? Josh spun around, frantic. "Mud Flap! Mud Flap!" he shouted. A gale of air snatched his words like feathers. She was gone!

He squinted into the ground blizzard. Nothing! Josh dropped his pack and bedroll and stumbled back into the meadow, dragging Pokey. A wall of wind pounded him, sending him sprawling. The cub squalled and rolled like a piece of tumbleweed on the leash, finally crouching, legs so wide his belly touched the ground. Josh tried to stand but was driven back down. He turned and groped toward his pack and bedroll, snow stinging his knees and hands. The wind howled madly, like an invisible monster trying to kill him.

Crawling, he conjured up images of the ranch, his parents, the motorcycle, and a warm fire. Again he heard the rifle blast and saw the bear fall. Then deep loneliness swallowed his thoughts. He closed his eyes and slowed his crawl. It would feel so good to lie down. He could curl up, and a big white blanket would cover him. Things would be all right.

He wished Dad were here to start a fire for him. He'd have wished for Tye, but Tye hadn't been as good with fires as Dad thought. Josh remembered the year before Tye's death. Dad had sent the two of them out into the trees above the ranch to try winter camping. He'd taught them everything they needed to know: to not work up a sweat, how to cut down pine boughs to sleep on, to wear layers of clothes, to stay dry, to eat well, and how to start a winter fire.

They had done everything right, but they couldn't get the fire started. Then Tye committed the big taboo. He pulled out some newspaper he'd smuggled along in his pack. He used paper to start the fire—he cheated! Dad had told them that if their life depended on a fire, there might not be paper hanging on a tree—so they needed to learn to use what nature provided.

What followed was a heated debate. Josh argued against cheating, but Tye insisted Dad would never find out. Tye was bigger so they ended up using the paper. Somehow the fire hadn't seemed very warm to Josh that night.

Many times Tye bragged to Dad about starting that fire in the snow—not mentioning how. Josh kept the secret after Tye's death, even when Dad got mad and bragged about Tye.

Something jerked his wrist, and Josh's eyes started open. The storm swarmed around him. Pokey had balked on the rope. Josh yanked back. "Come on, Pokey! Don't stop. We can't!" Something was burning at his arms and legs like a flame.

As Josh neared his pack, the angry wind held its breath so he could stand. He swung the pack to his back and tripped forward on numb feet, clutching the bedroll. Pokey trailed timidly, his body trembling in the wind. Higher on the slope, wind stirred the snow, sweeping it into tumbling clouds.

During a lull, Josh glimpsed an outcropping of rocks ahead, like a huge ship's bow thrust from the hillside. Closer yet, trees combed the slope. Josh plowed through the drifting snow, heading into the trees.

A dull crashing sound echoed closer and closer. Josh listened past the wind. The echo of splitting wood raced across the timbered slope. All over, trees were caving in before an onslaught of berserk wind. Deafening cracks drowned out the gale as trees snapped like matchsticks and crashed around Josh. He froze, eyes wide. Had the sky exploded?

Then came his worst nightmare. He half heard, half felt a splintering blast. A massive pine tree, not twenty feet away, began an awesome slow-motion plunge directly toward him. He stumbled backward, but the cub bolted across the fall line.

"No!" Josh shouted, yanking back as hard as he could.

The cub spun and twisted frantically. Then Josh slipped and hit the icy ground. Stunned, he watched with horror as the huge tree smashed across the taut leash, inches from his hand. The ground shook, and a branch smacked his face.

CHAPTER 11

CHAPTER

DEPUTY BREWSTER BINGHAM eyed the sky as he sped out of the McGuires' driveway. This storm defied the laws of nature. Ragged bolts of lightning forked into a black horizon. Icy pellets pounded the windshield. Lightning and snow—it wasn't right. Rules in nature, like rules in society, brought order. This storm disobeyed that order. Brewster grabbed for the handset. "Dispatch, this is Twenty-Two. Come in."

A pinched female voice sounded, "Roger, Twenty-Two. This is Dispatch, go ahead."

"Request directions to the residence of Otis Sinclair."

Brewster did not have to wait long for the dispatch to direct him. He interrupted her sign-off. "Dispatch, could you also patch me through to Sean O'Schanessy, Bozeman Search and Rescue?"

"Roger, Twenty-Two. Please hold."

Soon the radio crackled, "Twenty-Two, Mr. O'Schanessy is standing by."

"Roger, Dispatch, patch him through," Brewster answered. He enjoyed having Sean around at times like this. Sean worked as a volunteer for the Gallatin County Search and Rescue squad. Many citizens, as well as several officers, owed their lives to the outspoken volunteer. Though Brewster was in charge, this would be Sean's search.

A thick Irish voice crackled on the radio. "Hey! You looking for me?"

"Roger, Sean. Are you busy this fine afternoon?"

"Oh, not at all. I'm sunbathing till my wife shovels snow off me and drags me to the phone. What have we?"

Brewster smiled. The Irishman's bantering annoyed dispatchers. They didn't realize that for people on the front line, bantering was often emotional survival.

"Sean, I need your help," Brewster said. "We have a runaway boy, possibly headed into the Bridger Mountains."

"Why the mountains?"

"He's got a bear cub and a dog with him. Because of this storm, I'll have bulletins out within the hour. But if we don't hear anything by nightfall, you'd better expect the worst and have the men ready to go in after the storm."

"Did you say a bear cub? What's the child doing with—"

"Sean, meet me at the station in an hour. I'll explain."

"I'll be there, but you'd be wise to keep your socks pulled high. This storm here, she's a sassy one."

"Ten-four."

As Brewster drove toward Otis Sinclair's, his mind worked. He only had a few pieces of the puzzle—what was the big picture? When he returned to the station he would call Mrs. McGuire. If Sam harmed her, he'd—Brewster shook his head and swallowed hard. Emotions had little place in this type of work. This was a race against time. Emotions only stole precious seconds away from a young boy who needed help.

Pulling up to the isolated cabin, Brewster noticed all the keep-out signs. People liked privacy for different reasons. Some had things to hide, others things to protect. Some had bones to pick. Which was Otis?

A stiffening wind plucked at Brewster's sleeves and tie as he crawled from the patrol car. In the drive, an old green Ford Falcon sat forlornly. Rows of cages buttressed the cabin. Brewster spotted a thin man with wire-rimmed glasses feverishly nailing boards on the pens. The man looked a bit like a weathered professor—not old, maybe sixty, and hunched slightly. He glanced up with assessing eyes, and Brewster saw contempt in his craggy glare.

"Mr. Sinclair," Brewster called, approaching.

"Hand me some boards," the man ordered.

Brewster passed him two pieces of rough-cut barn wood. "Mr. Sinclair, I'm Deputy Bingham. I've got a few questions."

Otis kept nailing. "Officer, if you want to talk, grab a hammer and start covering these pens with me. This storm's not waiting for us to have tea."

Brewster bit at his bottom lip. "Your talkin' had better make it worth my while," he said, grabbing a hammer.

Otis Sinclair impressed Brewster. The recluse had a soft quality under his gruffness. Why had he barricaded himself out here alone? People usually looked for the company of other humans. Those who defied that compulsion had reason.

"Am I doing this right?" Brewster yelled into the wind as he nailed a board up on a chest-high cage. Behind the chicken wire a scrawny red fox paced nervously.

Otis looked directly at Brewster. "If it saves their lives, you're doing it right."

"Mr. Sinclair, I have some questions about the McGuire boy. Can you tell me what you know about him?"

Otis handed Brewster more boards before he spoke. "I know a lot about Josh, but I don't know where he's gone if that's what you're getting at. He lost a brother about a year ago, and his father, Sam, has taken to drinking since. Sam's not too fond of me. Suppose it's because he likes hunting and he sees Josh preferring to spend his time over here helping me save these fool animals of mine." Otis motioned to his left. "Nail something on that cage."

Brewster looked in at two raccoons huddling close, their bandit eyes barely open. "What's wrong with them?" he asked.

"Bullet wounds," Otis spit accusingly.

Brewster shook his head as he nailed. He knew as

well as anyone how one small bullet could destroy a life. "What do you do, Mr. Sinclair?" he asked.

"You're watching it. My name's Otis. Haven't been called Mr. Sinclair since I taught at the university."

"What did you teach?"

"They called it biology. I called it survival."

"Otis, can you tell me any more about Josh?"

The wiry man thought a moment. "Just one thing: he's got backbone. He'd crawl in any of these cages to help a wounded animal. Would you crawl in with that cat?" Otis asked, pointing to a snarling bobcat. The dust-white animal had its needle-sharp fangs bared and was hissing.

Brewster shook his head immediately.

Otis paused in his nailing. "What I'm saying is, don't be thinking Josh ran to the neighbor's barn. If he ran, I reckon as how he probably headed for the hills. Except for this storm, I'd be wishing you fools never found him.

Brewster held his tongue. Otis treated the whole world as his enemy. "Where do you want these last couple boards?" Brewster asked.

"Listen, Officer, unless you've got more questions, why don't you get! Josh needs your help more than me."

Brewster stared.

Otis waved his arms. "I said get! You need me to push your fancy patrol car out the drive?"

Brewster allowed a smile and waved Otis off. Crawling into his car he called back, "Good luck with the storm." Then he checked his watch and pulled sharply out of the driveway. So there it was: Otis's words against Sam McGuire's—pieces of a puzzle that didn't match. Which one did he throw out? Inside he already knew.

Pelting sleet made Brewster run for the door after arriving at the station. Once inside, he looked back at the sky. Darned if he'd ever seen anything like this. The gods were cooking up a dandy. He beat his gloved hands and kicked slush off his shoes.

Sean O'Schanessy stood waiting. Dirty work clothes failed to hide the brawny muscles of the short man's neck and arms. Sean looked like a human tugboat.

"Good to see you," Brewster said, extending his hand.

O'Schanessy's grip would have hefted a hundred-pound bag of cement. "This storm's forgetting her manners, huh," he said soberly.

Brewster nodded. "Sean, I've got some details for you, but the bottom line is, I think the boy's run to the mountains."

O'Schanessy walked slowly over to a window and peered out. When he spoke, reverence edged his voice. "If the laddy has, Lord have mercy."

CHAPTER 12

CHAPTER

JOSH STRUGGLED to his knees, rubbing his bruised jaw. Something tasted sweet. Why had he come to this place? First he'd lost Mud Flap. And now the cub was dead—crushed. He swallowed over and over. He had killed Pokey and Mud Flap.

A noise, little more than a faint cry, pitched with the wind. Josh cocked his head to listen. It kept breaking abruptly, like a bleating or bawling sound. At times it sounded close—very close. Could it be? Legs shaking, Josh scrambled over the log.

There was Pokey, his small eyes dancing with fear, squalling and struggling, frantically raking brown patches of dirt up through the deepening snow.

"Pokey, it's okay now. Easy, I won't hurt you."

The cub looked wild eyed at the tree and let out a tense bawl. Then it struggled again, becoming a blurred bundle of grunting, twisting hair.

Josh grabbed the rope and pulled, straining to free the cub. Stubbornly, in short jerks, the rope slid from under the tree. One last yank broke it free, tumbling both of them backward into snow as deep as the cub's legs. Once free of the tree, the cub quit struggling. It panted heavily, its little chest heaving and trembling.

Josh should have been happy, but something was wrong. His face and hands had stopped burning. A strange numbness now made his limbs feel wooden, and he kept wanting to lie down in the snow and quit.

Josh sensed in that moment something fearful and urgent. Struggling to stand, he teetered on his legs. He shuffled his feet and swung his arms but felt nothing, not even the leash. What if Pokey escaped? With clumsy movements Josh snugged the rope tightly to his wrist. He had to find shelter and crawl into the sleeping bag. Then again, maybe it would be okay to curl up on the open ground.

"No!" Josh screamed at himself, his voice hoarse and shrill. He stared wildly about. The trees weren't safe—he'd be crushed. He brushed a numb hand across his lips and found red on his fingers. The red meant nothing. Josh shifted his pack and clutched his bag, trudging forward. The rocks ahead were his only hope.

A jerk on the rope reminded him he was leading Pokey. He turned. The cub had balked, his button eyes glinting. The wind ruffled his piled hair. Josh yanked hard, bouncing Pokey forward on his short, stiff peg legs. The cub started bawling again, his cry pitched with panic. Josh ignored it. He couldn't stop now, not for Pokey, not for the storm, not for anything.

Wind stung his eyes. Back and forth along the bouldered ridge he searched—where could he go? The biggest rocks stood alone, offering little protection. His strength had seeped from his body like water from a rusty bucket. Soon the bucket would be empty. And then what?

Josh headed toward the largest group of boulders. Snow caked his pants nearly to the knees, but he felt nothing. Whatever happened, he'd soon go no farther.

Approaching the rocks, his heart sank. The boulders had large gaps between them. He staggered in among them, bumping clumsily off the rocks like a steel ball in a giant pinball machine. Josh tried not to panic, but now his feet refused to lift from the snow. Vaguely he recognized a dark, flat rock and knew he had come a full circle. His shuffling stopped. Above him the wind screamed and wailed madly like cats fighting in the sky. The cub huddled against his ankles.

"I'm sorry, Pokey," Josh said. His voice sounded weak and raspy.

The cub tucked his buff-colored nose down against his belly and curled up in the snow. Pokey was doing what was right, Josh thought. It was time to huddle by a rock and go to sleep. He actually felt warm now. He thought of opening his sleeping bag, but his hands didn't move so good—he'd be okay. If only he wasn't so tired. He let his body slump to the ground next to Pokey. The bundled sleeping bag dropped in the snow, and his gaze drifted. It felt peaceful.

As he relaxed, his head started nodding. His gaze drifted, looking at the world in slow motion. Something struck him as odd. To his right about twenty feet, two rocks wedged against each other. A thick bush grew at the bottom. Josh stared, thinking, So what?

He felt the cub shiver next to him. That wasn't right. Pokey shouldn't be cold. The cub should be warm and tired. It bothered Josh that the cub was shivering, and he looked again at the bush. He strained to get to his feet but they didn't work. At last he fell forward on his stomach and floundered in the snow. With the pack still on his back, and dragging the sleeping bag, he awkwardly wiggled over to the shrub. The cub trailed close.

Josh's arms moved with spastic jerks, no longer obeying well. This was it—soon his bucket would be empty. Flailing and clawing at the shrub, he lowered his head and peered under. Darkness—what did that mean? His thoughts muddled. Was it a bear's den? Or maybe a mountain lion's? He had to crawl into the menacing black space.

He stared long. Maybe it would be better to just lie down here by the shrub. No! He had to crawl forward. Over and over he repeated the thought. Still he did not move. Suddenly the wind pitched to a wild scream, and Pokey bolted past, burrowing under the branches. Josh held his breath, listening for some terrible snarl or roar. Nothing. Fumbling with the branches, he squirmed in behind the cub. The small, dark cavity was like being in a big garbage can, with barely room to move his pack and bag. Outside the storm's madness grew muffled.

As the cub watched, Josh clawed open the bedroll. Without coaxing, the cub wiggled into the unrolled bag and disappeared to the bottom. Josh could not sit up, nor could he stretch out. Several times he banged his head on the rock as he tried to squirm into the bag after Pokey. Finally he had the bag around him. He fumbled to pull the top closed. A sharp pain gripped his stomach, and he curled on his side, knees pulled up to his chest.

Pokey, wet and quivering, huddled against Josh's shins. The wind howled mournfully, and Josh started to shiver and could not stop.

Josh's mother sat up alone. All evening she stayed near the phone, listening to the radio and watching the TV. The deputy, Brewster Bingham, had been good about calling her that afternoon. It bothered her, someone checking up like that—this was her house. And yet, she had asked that he call.

Each hour the radio and TV station reported Josh's disappearance, along with details—more details than Sam would like. Whenever the phone rang, Libby picked it up trembling. So far it was only well-wishers wondering if she had heard anything.

It angered her when Sam headed up to bed early. How could he sleep when his child was missing? Three hours of hearing the bed creak, however, assured her that Sam was still awake.

After midnight, Libby called the sheriff's office. "Hello, this is Libby McGuire," she said. "Have you heard anything yet?"

"I'm sorry, we haven't." The man's voice was patient. "We've had lots of phone calls, but no one's seen him. KUTV in Salt Lake City and Channel Four in Billings both called."

"Why?" Libby asked.

"Requesting information. They're getting lots of calls asking about your boy and his bear."

"Please let me know if you hear anything," she begged.

"We will, Mrs. McGuire. We're doing all we can. When the storm lets up, the search crews will head in. Until then, we can only wait. Get some sleep— tomorrow could be a long day."

"Okay," she murmured. "Thanks." Libby hung up knowing the man was right. But she also knew she'd sleep precious little until Josh came home.

Brewster Bingham was already up when the five-thirty alarm rang. Most of the night he had tossed and turned, listening to the wind howl. Every time it pitched, it seemed to chip away at his hope. Not until four o'clock had the storm's urgency slackened. If the boy was out in this weather, he'd be dead. But they would still search to find the body.

Brewster winced as he limped on his stiff leg. Cold weather played havoc with the bum limb. He started the coffee perking. Today he'd fill his thermos full. Who knew where he might end up.

Several inches of slushy snow made it slippery tromping out to his car. Slate-gray clouds hung low, hiding the dawn. If there was this much snow in the valley, what must it be like in the mountains?

First he stopped by the station. Already Sean was

there calling the Sheriff's Posse members. Brewster made a quick call to Scott Air Force Base. They were the ones who would dispatch the local Civil Air Patrol Club for an air search. Two more calls put the local Nordic Ski Club and Snowmobile Club on alert in case they were needed.

Brewster wanted to stop by the McGuires' before search crews headed out—to check on Libby McGuire and also to talk to her husband again. Brewster had noticed something yesterday. In Sam McGuire's eyes there had been many things: anger, frustration, fear. But not evil.

"Sean," he said, "hold the fort down. I'll be back soon."

"You'd be going to breakfast without me?"

Brewster smiled. "I'm heading to the McGuires'."

"Step light . . . I know that Sam. He's a good man, but shy on luck. You mustn't corner him."

Brewster nodded. "He might be cornering himself," he said.

Heading out, the roads were wet and sloppy. When Brewster pulled in the drive, the ranch yard stood empty. He drew a deep breath and crawled stiffly from the patrol car. The air held an eerie calm, as if resting from its night of anger. As Brewster approached the house, he adjusted his belt. Mrs. McGuire was peering out the window. By the time he reached the porch, she had the door open.

"Have you found him?" she asked, her voice tense with hope.

"Not yet, but search teams are headed up this

morning. The Civil Air Patrol will be flying search patterns on these western slopes. The snow will melt quickly, but if we find tracks, the Nordic and Snowmobile clubs are ready. Normally we don't gear up into a full-scale search this fast, but with the storm last night, we can't take any chances."

"Please come in," Libby said, her eyes red and hollowed. She had the haunted look of someone nearing her limit.

"Are you doing okay?" Brewster asked, stepping inside. He noticed her desperately toying with a button on her blouse.

"I'm worried," she said.

"Mrs. McGuire, we—"

"Call me Libby."

"Libby, we'll find him," Brewster said, not voicing his deeper suspicions. "Is Sam here?"

"Upstairs. Should I call him?"

"Please."

As Libby hurried off, Brewster looked around. The living room was like a thousand others he'd been in, except for the pictures on the mantel and wall. Yet it was those pictures—the wedding pictures, the young boys holding up their first fish, children sitting on their parents' laps in front of Christmas trees—it was those pictures that made each home special. Brewster stood to look at the photographs. They showed happiness, laughing, hugging, kissing, holding, and teasing. Not a one hinted at the McGuires' desperate hell.

"Find anything?" Sam McGuire asked.

The coarse voice surprised Brewster. Sam stood, looking as if he hadn't slept in days. Rough stubble shaded his jaw and surrounded his dried and cracked lips. Brewster noted Sam's hands shaking. Libby stood close behind, still pulling at the button.

"You have a nice family, Mr. McGuire," Brewster said.

"You wouldn't know," Sam rasped. "Did you find our son yet?"

"Not yet," Brewster said.

Sam's voice grew cold. "Why aren't you out looking?"

"What are you so angry about?" Brewster asked.

"My boy's run away. Isn't that enough?"

"Anger won't find him," Brewster said. "Thinking might."

"Why don't you just leave us alone," Sam spit.

"I'm here to help. What's wrong with that?"

"Everyone in five counties knows about us now, thanks to you."

"And everyone is helping look," Brewster added.

"Baloney! They could care less."

Brewster winced. "I know what you're—"

"You know nothin'. You come in here talking big. Without that uniform, you ain't diddily."

Accustomed to weighing his words carefully, Brewster for once threw out the scales. He took a step forward. "Now I'll tell you something, Mr. McGuire. Your son could be on the mountain this very minute, dead or freezing to death. And look at you, sitting here feeling sorry for yourself."

Libby still fidgeted with her button. Suddenly it popped off and caromed across the floor. She burst into tears and chased after it. Sam ignored her, and for an instant Brewster expected him to come out swinging. Instead Sam turned and walked to the window.

"What do you want?" he asked, his voice hollow and weak.

"The same thing as you," Brewster said. "I want to find your son. I'm not feeling much like left-handed compliments, but from what I gather, you've got one hell of a boy. Good kids don't just happen, Mr. McGuire. Like father—like son."

Sam turned to look at Brewster, blinking his eyes. "Tye shouldn't have died."

"I've heard about Tye. No, you're right," Brewster allowed. "I don't suppose he should have. But now Josh is in trouble. It's him you have to think about."

Sam rocked on his heels and tilted his head back, as if resting his thoughts.

"How is Josh at starting fires?" Brewster asked.

Sam turned away and hung his head.

"Mr. McGuire. Can he start a fire?"

"I don't know. I tried so hard to teach him. He just didn't . . . well, have much knack for it like Tye. Officer, I . . . I don't know what to do."

"You can start by telling me how Josh thinks. What's in his head—I don't know him."

Sam rocked forward, his voice subdued. "Not sure I do either, Officer."

CHAPTER

CHAPTER 13

WRAPPED INSIDE his sleeping bag, Josh awoke to an eerie silence. His thoughts drifted in and out of sleep, and he stretched at his drowsiness. Other feelings came slowly. His jaw still hurt. Hot burning touched his cheeks and fingers. And the sleeping bag felt cold and clammy. He shivered, huddling with his knees pulled to his chest. There was warmth—not that he could feel, but a lack of the bitter cold he remembered too well.

Something smelled awful. He wrinkled his nose and tried to swallow. A sharp knot twisted his stomach. Loud, rhythmic clucking hummed nearby. The sound seemed to pulse with a pain in his hand—something was sucking on his thumb! He jerked. Sharp pins gripped his wrist and held tightly. The sucking became frantic. What in the world? He reached his other hand over and felt. Warm, furry hair vibrated and pulsed with the clucking sound. Pokey, it was Pokey—he must be hungry.

Josh let Pokey keep his right hand, painfully working open the sleeping bag. Fresh air washed across his face. At first it appeared dark, but dim light filtered through the shrubbed opening. The air had lost its bite and seemed to warm even as he reached for the snow-covered pack near the opening. The effort made his fingertips burn, especially the thumb being sucked on. It wasn't cold now, so why did his fingers hurt so bad? He yanked his right hand away from Pokey.

Like lightning, Pokey lunged and bit his wrist. Then the cub clung tightly to the hand, his needle-sharp claws digging deep.

"Ouch, Pokey!" Josh said, struggling. Then he slacked his hurting arm, too weak to fight. Pokey relaxed his claws and returned to sucking the thumb. If Josh did anything, it would have to be with his left hand. Nobody was stealing that thumb from Pokey. And still something smelled terrible.

Josh used his teeth and left hand to dig open his pack. His fingers stung and moved awkwardly. Sucking, the cub gazed intently. Josh removed the feeding bottle, glad he had filled it at home. Ice sloshed around and made the plastic cold. He offered the bottle, but Pokey refused to give up the thumb. Josh squeezed some of the milk-egg mixture in the side of the cub's lips. Pokey sucked so hard his baby teeth dug into the thumb.

"Dang it! You're eating my thumb, Pokey. Please . . . here!" Josh shoved the nipple alongside his thumb and started squeezing a steady stream of fluid into the suckling mouth. At the same time, he drew his thumb slowly away. It worked. Pokey made happy, sharp grunts, slurping at the cold liquid. The cub reached and held onto the bottle with his paws.

Josh wondered why his own stomach kept knotting. Was it from the bad smell? What was that smell anyway? He peered under the bush at the calm gray sky. Was it morning or evening? He tried to remember when he'd last eaten—the night he left home, but how long ago was that? It seemed years since he'd watched the lights go out in the house and pushed the cycle out the drive, starting this dumb trip with Pokey and Mud Flap.

Mud Flap—he'd forgotten about her. "Mud Flap! Mud Flap! Here, Mud Flap!" he shouted. His voice muffled in the dark hole. Where was she? She'd disappeared in the snow, and then what? If she froze, would he find her stiff body? It was his fault. He had let her come along. Thinking of Mud Flap left Josh sick, and the rotten odor made it worse. Then he found what caused the awful smell—Pokey had messed in the bag. Josh felt weak and nauseated. He retched a couple of times, but nothing came up. Maybe food would help.

Josh reached into the pack for a candy bar. Leaving the wrapper on, he took a bite. He ignored the wax paper and gnawed away. Without water, his throat caked, and he choked. Why hadn't he filled the canteen up a little? He couldn't swallow the bite.

He wanted to grab the cub's bottle and squeeze some of the precious liquid into his own mouth, but he remembered Pokey's anger. Josh ran his hand across the pack and scraped off snow. Handful after handful he ate the white slush. It melted slowly and brought back his chill. Painfully he bit off another stiff chunk of candy bar and forced a swallow. Each mouthful steadied his movements and thoughts. By the last bite, he thought to take off the wrapper. The snow made his teeth hurt.

Josh stared at the small traces of light filtering in, and his thoughts wandered. What were his parents doing now? Had they gotten a storm like this in Bozeman? If so, were they worried about him? And how were Otis's animals—especially the big owl? The thoughts made him homesick. He felt so alone. He wished Tye were here, but Tye was gone—real gone!

Memories of his brother haunted Josh and reminded him of Mookee Man. He could hear his dad's voice whispering the tale of Mookee Man in the glow of a late-night campfire.

"Once upon a time in the land of Wanabee people," his father would say secretively, his voice hushed, "there lived Mookee Man. Now Wanabee people were wonderful and did anything they could dream. They rode the wind and chased the moon. They sang songs to make sunsets brighter. They traveled through time. They even tasted colors and saw smells. They had only one problem."

"What was that?" Josh whispered each time, even though he'd heard the answer a hundred times.

"Mookee Man!" His father hissed the name wickedly, glancing over his shoulder into the dark.

Josh cuddled closer to his dad and looked fearfully into the darkness himself. "Tell me about him," he begged.

"Well . . . okay. You see, Mookee Man was a devil. He hated Wanabee people and tried to steal happiness from them. He told lies and offered worthless trinkets and cheap knickknacks."

"Why, Dad?"

"Who knows—that even puzzled the Wanabees. If they wanted worthless trinkets and cheap knick-knacks, they could wish them into being, mountains of them. In fact, the happiness Mookee Man tried to steal could have been his for free if he'd only joined the Wanabees."

"Why didn't he?" Josh asked.

"Because he was lazy and foolish . . . without character. Remember, nobody knows about the Wanabees anymore except you and Mamma and Tye and me. It's our secret, Josh. Okay?"

Josh nodded, feeling privileged.

"And remember, Josh. Mookee Man is still around. He isn't one person. He's anyone in our family who's cruel, or lies, or cheats. Mookee Man is the one of us who does what is wrong."

Over the years, Dad had told him and Tye the same story many different ways. Resting now beside the cub, Josh worried. Had everything he'd done leaving home made him Mookee Man?

After finishing the bottle, the cub relaxed. It curled against Josh's stomach and licked its front paws con-tentedly. The small body felt warm and vibrated with rhythmic clucking. Josh hugged the cub as light trickled in brighter from the outside—it must be morning.

"Pokey, we're going to be all right. We've just got to find a better place and get a fire going." Josh swallowed hard. "We've got to find Mud Flap, too," he said. "And, oh yeah, I better hide the cycle." He worked his tender hands open and closed. "Pokey, why are my fingers so sore?"

He looked at his hands but saw no cuts or scrapes. The cub still sucked its paw, and Josh relaxed. He tried to think of everything he should do, but his thoughts jumbled and he stared down in a daze. A beam of sunlight peeked through and glinted off Pokey's woolly ears.

As they cuddled, Josh felt warmth from the fuzzy black body. Otis explained once how different animals have different body temperatures. If so, bears must be real warm. Remembering the snowstorm, he wondered if maybe Pokey had saved his life.

Josh was tempted to roll over and fall back to sleep. But he had chores to do. Having to start a fire bothered him, especially after this snow. Why were fires so hard to start? This time he didn't have his father along, or Tye with his newspaper. This time he wasn't near home, and it wasn't for practice. He had to start a fire—all alone!

Josh kneeled in the small space and shooed Pokey out of the bag. Then he wiped and shook out the stinky mess as best he could. His fingers stung. Everything he wore was damp. He'd been too cold to take his shoes off when he crawled in. Josh was glad his dad didn't know how stupid he'd been. Nobody went to bed in wet clothes and shoes.

Shielding his eyes, Josh crawled under the bush into the open. Morning sun broke through the clouds and glistened on a layer of wet snow. Josh squinted. For a moment he turned his body toward the sun, wallowing in the warmth. Everything seemed so different. It took a moment to recognize the flat area where he'd left the cycle. Broken trees were scattered along the slope where Pokey had nearly been hit. Josh left his bedroll and pack on a rock and tied Pokey to a shrub, then headed for the motorcycle.

He called for Mud Flap as he walked, working his way through the shin-deep snow. When he came to where the cycle should have been, it was gone. He breathed fast, searching frantically. Who could have found the cycle and taken it during the storm? Then he spotted a handlebar sticking out of a snowdrift. He sighed. The cycle had tipped over in the wind. Josh hoped it hadn't lost too much gas. He kicked snow from around the Honda, then reached down and grabbed hold. It lifted stiff and heavy.

First he tried pushing the cycle toward the grove of trees, but the big machine refused to move uphill through snow. Josh doubted it would start either. Besides, he felt too weak. Instead he rolled it downhill, jumping on and steering into a ravine. The deep tracks showed clearly in the snow.

He'd never get the bike back up again without starting it. Of course, if it didn't start, what use was it? He rested the kickstand on a solid stone and then broke branches, piling them around the tires and on top of the gas tank. Unless a person walked near, they wouldn't see the cycle once the snow melted. And that wouldn't be long judging by the big globs of wet snow melting and plopping from the trees.

Josh found a trickle of water flowing through the tall grass. He kneeled down and drank the icy water until pain pinched his head—that always happened when he drank something cold.

He hollered at the top of his voice as he walked back toward Pokey. "Mud Flap! Mud Flap! Here, girl . . . come here, girl." He pressed his thumb and forefinger into his mouth to whistle, the same way he called cows at home. His tender jaw and the burning in his fingertips allowed only a rough spitting sound. He stared down. His fingers were red and puffy on the ends. They hurt like his ears and nose when he touched them.

Every time he heard a big clump of snow fall, Josh turned expectantly. Where was Mud Flap? He kept heading toward Pokey, searching as he went. Maybe he would find her tracks. He also looked for someplace to hide. In the meadow someone might find him. But he dared not climb too high on the peak. If another storm came, he'd never find protection up there. He examined the hillside.

His gaze rested on a dark hollow in the side of the mountain. Actually he saw several holes marking the steep slope, but one looked bigger than the rest and was hidden behind a buttress of rocks. Unless someone looked from this side of the meadow, the space would not be visible. He noticed a stand of trees crowding the bottom of the rocky face. That could provide firewood.

Josh shouldered his pack, then grabbed the bag and Pokey's leash. The hole looked nearly a quarter mile off, and the snow made the going slow. All the while Josh kept yelling for Mud Flap. Even Pokey seemed to know why Josh was calling. He kept turning his little head side to side, eyes flickering and moving as he bounced along. Every few steps he swatted at the snow playfully or rolled a somersault. Once he tackled Josh's feet and sent him sprawling in the snow. Josh could only laugh as the cub wiggled with excitement.

Hiking through the slushy snow numbed Josh's feet, but the rest of him warmed. Halfway to the trees, he spotted tracks angling in a big arc to his left. They were probably from a deer. On the chance they might be Mud Flap's, he hiked toward them. Drawing closer, Pokey quit his playing and started shoving his short front legs stiffly in front of his walk. Small dribbles of yellow urine peppered the snow behind his hind legs. Then his little body froze as he sniffed a track.

The big prints—larger than Josh's—showed claws and had heel marks like a human's. Josh caught his breath. Dogs, deer, elk—nothing walked flat-footed that he'd ever seen. Nothing that is, except bear. He studied the prints. Nervously he looked around—maybe it wasn't bear. He'd never seen a bear track that big. He looked closer. The marks showed the animal's toes were reversed. The little toe marks were on the inside, and the big toe marks were on the outside of each print. Josh didn't remember bear's toes being on backward.

"Come here, Pokey," he called. He pulled Pokey in and lifted him carefully to look at his hind feet. Pokey's toes were on backward. "Cripes, Pokey, let's get out of here!" Josh stuttered.

CHAPTER 14

CHAPTER

JOSH STUMBLED away from the tracks as fast as he could and headed toward the cave. Pokey kept up, bobbing up and down in the snow. The last hundred yards were steep and dangerous because of the wet slush and sharp rocks. Josh watched the ground carefully as he climbed. Every few steps his feet slipped and he grabbed for handholds. The climb would have been hard even without pack, bedroll, and cub.

Pokey had no trouble following. At times he even scampered ahead on the leash, actually pulling. When Josh stopped to rest, he looked back. The meadow was really a basin, surrounded on three sides by Ram's Horn Peak, a ridge line, and another smaller peak he couldn't name. The large bear tracks were still visible, angling into the lower valley. Josh swallowed hard and kept going.

The hole in the rock looked different up close. It loomed large, spreading nearly thirty feet across the face of the steep slope, then narrowing quickly inward, ending after only fifteen feet. The rear of the cave formed a small cubbyhole the size of a pup tent.

This wasn't a true cave, it was more a big pocket. Breathing heavily, Josh dropped his pack and bag on the dry, protected ground. No one could see him from above or below. He would drag branches up so even an airplane couldn't spot him. He didn't know how well he'd be protected from the wind, though. "What do you think, Pokey?" he asked.

The cub ignored him and sniffed back and forth, nosing into every nook and crack of the hollow. Josh pulled out several pieces of jerky and bread and wolfed them down. The cub started grunting and sniffing around Josh for a handout. Josh surrendered some jerky. Then he tied Pokey to a big rock and headed back down the slope to get water.

He filled the canteen and took it up to Pokey. From a natural bowl in a rock, Pokey slurped at the water. Next Josh carried up armloads of branches. Would he ever get a fire going? He tried not to think about it as he broke limbs off standing dead trees—they were much drier than ground wood from under the wet snow. Then he went lower in the trees and hunted for kindling.

As he searched, he thought of all the times he'd needed help starting a fire. Josh swore his dad could touch a match to a whole log and get a flame going. Dad wasn't a cheater. And neither was he, Josh thought. Lots of times he could have used paper without Dad knowing. But the fire would have known; fires knew things like that.

Most of these trees were jack pine—called scrub pine, on account of how tall and straight they grew with only a scrub's worth of growth at the top. At the bottom, small dried branches grew like whiskers. It was these "weenie" branches Josh looked for. He didn't understand why or how the small toothpicks of wood could be dead when the tree was still alive, but they were. Dad called it squaw wood. The noodle-thin ends were gray and gnarled, free of any bark to hold moisture. Most were bone dry, protected by the upper growth.

Patiently Josh worked tree to tree, gathering tinder. When a twig bent without breaking, he discarded it. Only an immediate snap meant the wood was dry. Josh filled both fists and headed back up the slope. Had the ground not been wet, he could have looked for leaves or pine needles.

Inside the hollow, he fell to his knees. If he could start a fire, the smoke would be broken up by the overhang. Carefully he wedged a handful of tiny twigs up against a cup-sized rock. The breeze blew lightly. Protecting the wood with his body, Josh pulled the book of matches from his pack. Why hadn't he brought more? These weren't even the big farmer's matches you could strike anywhere. Instead he had the kind that opened up, like grocery stores hand out.

Fingers trembling, Josh ripped out and struck a match against the black edge. A small spark blinked, but the match refused to light. Was it damp? He struck another match. This one fizzled out as quickly. Match after match Josh tried. One stayed lit but went out as he forced it under the twigs. Another flared but blew out when the breeze gusted.

Josh knew if he'd had paper now he would have cheated. In fact, maybe he did have some. Could he burn some of the money he'd stuffed in his pants before leaving home? Just the dollars. He reached in his blue jeans. As soon as his fingers touched the wet clump of bills he knew it was useless.

Dad always said starting a fire was easy. A flame wanted to burn if you let it, but impatience usually snuffed it out. Failure drifted like a big shadow over Josh's thoughts as he struck another match. If only it was that easy. He couldn't even light money—how bad was that? He fought back tears as the new match flared and stayed lit.

Josh stared, tempted to shove the taunting flame quickly under the twigs. Instead he tipped the match. As the flame grew, he crowded it with his body, protecting it. When the yellow reached his fingers, Josh leveled the match and moved it under the nest of twigs. The flame crept closer and closer to his fingers. Still he waited. The flame wavered and spit, and Josh felt heat against his fingers but dared not drop the match—he had only three left and they might be damp. One small twig glowed and passed its flame to another. He held his breath so his hand wouldn't shake. But the flame bit his finger, and he dropped the match with a jerk.

He watched the match burn out. But still there glowed a tiny tongue of flame. Several times it shriveled and flickered. Josh bent over and blew ever so lightly—any harder would make the leaf of light disappear. Soon a small stream of yellow and blue snaked up through the twigs, wafting smoke. He wanted to jump up, shouting and laughing. Instead he held his breath and fed twigs to the fire one by one.

Only when the flames licked up a full foot did Josh relax. This would be a good fire, a real fire, an honest fire. He held his hands out to the flame, even though the air was warm and he was hot from climbing. Maybe he could warm his memories of the bitter storm. Something he could not warm away were his memories of Mud Flap. She couldn't have made it through the storm—she didn't have a sleeping bag.

The sun blazed high above. Dark clouds from the storm had drifted to the east, leaving clear blue sky. Pokey, full of food, was possessed with energy. Bounding in circles around the rock, he bucked with excitement. Over and over he rolled somersaults. When he stood up he shook his head so hard he threw himself over, then sat up with a look of embarrassment. Josh laughed at Pokey's antics. It couldn't be wrong fighting to keep something so neat alive. How could anyone kill Pokey?

Josh felt alive, too, and started peeling off his wet clothes, even his underwear. Naked, he grabbed the cub's leash off the rock and started running circles around the fire. Josh howled with laughter and abandon. Pokey picked up on the game. Taking turns, they chased each other back and forth across the opening. Finally Josh collapsed, giggling. He breathed fast, his skinny legs and pale washboard ribs trembling and shaking. "I won't let anyone kill you, Pokey," Josh gasped loudly. The cub wiggled in reply, then pounced.

Every time Pokey tackled him, Josh rolled him over and tickled him. The cub squirmed with delight. His black button eyes glinted and danced in the sun. Finally, exhausted, the cub lay down to sleep by the fire.

Josh fed a couple chunks of wood to the flames, then went about spreading his clothes out to dry. He couldn't help worrying when he looked at the fire. What if it went out? How long would his food last? And would the game warden consider letting him keep Pokey and change the hunting laws? If not, he was never going home.

That thought made Josh lonely again, and he missed his mom and dad. Not the dad who swore at him and hit him, but the one who used to carry him on his shoulders for horseback rides. The one who bit a piece of twine in the middle so Josh had reins to steer him. Dad used to sit around fires like this and whittle out toys. He said every piece of wood had a toy inside if you whittled away the extra wood. Josh looked at the fire and wondered what toys he was burning.

A sharp sound in the noon air caught Josh's attention. A distinct yip echoed up from the meadow. Josh ran over and looked down. Nothing moved. Then he heard the sharp noise more clearly. Still he didn't recognize it. Suddenly he saw it. Far down across the meadow, bouncing up and down through the snow, was a small black-and-white animal.

CHAPTER 15

CHAPTER

"MUD FLAP! Mud Flap!" Josh screamed.

The black-and-white animal paused, looking around.

"Mud Flap! Is that you, girl?" Josh waved his arms.

It was Mud Flap, and she spotted him, leaping forward. She tucked her head and raced up the hill. Josh ran and met her, catching and spinning her. Her hair was matted and dirty. For nearly a half hour he cried and hugged the dog. She wiggled and squirmed in his arms, thumping her tail and licking his face.

Josh had no idea how Mud Flap had survived, but even Pokey seemed excited to see her. Back in camp, the two sniffed each other, Pokey grunting and Mud Flap whining. Feeling sorry for them, Josh fed Mud Flap and Pokey all they could eat. They gulped down bread, pancake dough, and jerky. Josh even broke open the can of tomato soup.

Afterward the two began playing in the warm sun. They scampered around, spinning and nipping and looking like they might hurt each other—but neither wanted to quit. While the animals played, Josh hiked down to the stream and washed his sleeping bag. The snow was melting fast, and Josh took off his shirt to soak in the sun. Back at the cave he spread all his wet belongings out on the boulders to dry.

As the afternoon wore on, the animals' play slowed until at last they laid down and gently pawed each other. Josh relaxed next to them and joined in the gentle shoving and pushing. Soon Pokey and Mud Flap fell fast asleep. Josh smiled. Running away wasn't really so bad.

The first night's stay in the cave lasted forever. Pokey and Mud Flap huddled together and whimpered through the night. Always fearful his precious fire might go out, Josh slept little, adding wood every hour. He really didn't like keeping the fire going at night. Someone might see it from the distance. But memory of the hard-to-start fire, and of the storm, convinced Josh he had no choice.

He also thought about something else. His parents would be worried sick about him because of the storm. His mom, especially, would be crying. He hated it when she cried. He hated it when anyone cried. Dad never cried, and Tye always said crying was sissy. Josh decided he wouldn't need to tell them where he was—just let them know not to worry.

There were other problems. He shouldn't have let Mud Flap and Pokey eat all they wanted yesterday, even if he had felt sorry for them. Together they had devoured all the pancake mix, soup, oatmeal, and bread as fast as Josh fed them. Now it was all gone, and Mud Flap ran her nose back and forth across the pack, whining.

"There's no more food, girl. I'm sorry," Josh said. He hung his head to avoid the two silver-black eyes that peered at him, wanting. His stomach churned with the same hunger. The only food left was some of Pokey's mix. Maybe he should give up and go home? "No!" Josh blurted aloud. He hated that thought. "We're not going home."

Determined and scared, he jumped to his feet. With Pokey and Mud Flap trailing behind, Josh headed down to the meadow to look for yampah. His father had taught him you could eat roots of the white plant. They were like miniature inch-long carrots. The slushy snow was nearly gone. Only small white patches clung to the shaded side of a few trees. After two hours of effort, Josh found barely a dozen yampah, and these were small and bitter. Neither of the animals would eat them.

Next Josh grabbed his fishing line and headed toward the ridge. From there it would be a two-mile hike down to Ram's Horn Lake. During the climb, Pokey and Mud Flap chased and bit playfully at each other. Josh wanted to stop and join the fun, but he had to find food.

From the notch between the peaks, he spotted the lake. Smoke curled up from a camp on the distant shore. Unlike the basin on the back side of the mountain, this small mountain lake was popular among campers. Maybe tomorrow nobody would be around, but for now he was out of luck.

The skinny of it, like his dad used to say, was he didn't bring enough food. And the only thing Josh could think to do was get the cycle going and chance a trip into Gardiner. The town sat near Yellowstone Park, maybe a dozen miles from where the gravel road into Tom Miner Basin met the highway.

He'd be safer going to Gardiner than to the lake. At the lake, even without the cub, it would seem odd to see a boy all alone. In town he'd be just another person. Riding by himself, he wouldn't draw attention. He could even park the cycle near the edge of town so he didn't have to ride in heavy traffic. The idea seemed dumb, but the hungrier Josh grew, the more he knew he had to do it. He looked up at the sky and guessed it to be early afternoon.

First he stoked the fire well. Then, after tying Pokey and Mud Flap to the big rock guarding the edge of the opening, he headed for the cycle. He hoped the animals would be okay. The afternoon sun sent a warm breeze drifting off the mountain. Josh carried the emptied pack along and wore every piece of clothing he had. Even when he found himself sweating, he refused to take anything off.

The cycle rested in the ravine where he'd left it. He pulled the branches away and picked up a stick, poking it in the gas tank. Only an inch of wet showed on the wood, hardly enough to make it into Gardiner. If he got the cycle started and out of the ravine, maybe he could shut the engine off and coast. It was mostly downhill the first four or five miles.

Josh's ears and fingers stung when he slid the helmet on. He ignored the pain and pulled out the choke, easing the engine over a couple of times. Then, with his tongue bunched between his teeth, he jumped hard on the kick starter. On the third try, the motor sputtered, then screamed to life, ripping the air. Josh wished he could stuff leaves or something in the exhaust. He let the engine run a bit, then gunned the throttle and raced up the short slope onto the meadow. Immediately he shut the engine off and coasted down across the grass toward the trail.

Riding down in daylight without the animals was easy, except for places where snowmelt left the trail slippery. Everything looked different by day. Near the road, Josh started the engine and rode past a small hunting cabin. He saw it had electricity and also a propane tank. Maybe there was food he could borrow. No, that would be stealing. He gunned the throttle and kept going. Soon he pulled onto the paved highway and headed south toward Gardiner.

Something surprised Josh: except for the thought of running out of gas, he wasn't scared. Remembering how terrified he'd been heading out that first night, now he felt numb to the fear. He tipped the helmet forward on his head and rode boldly—at least until he pulled into a gas station on the edge of Gardiner. Then a lump formed in his throat. He avoided talk with anyone while he pumped gas. It only cost a dollar to fill the small tank. Then he parked the cycle by the curb and headed for a pay phone.

He pulled the change from his pocket and started to dial home. If Dad answered he'd be furious. Memory of his father's anger stopped Josh. Hand shaking, he hung up the phone and stared at it. Try as he might, he couldn't find courage to pick it back up. Then a thought occurred to him.

Quickly he looked up Otis's number and dialed. A machine's voice instructed him to deposit a dollar eighty. Hand still shaking, Josh fumbled the coins into the slot. When he heard the ringing, his breath shortened. Whose side was Otis on? Otis might be angry he ran away and want to find him. But still Josh let the phone keep ringing, his hands sweating. Otis might refuse to give Dad a message—Dad hated Otis, and Otis knew it. As Josh prepared to give up, he heard a click.

"What?" came the gruff voice.

Josh's voice broke. "Otis . . . this is Josh," he stammered.

CHAPTER 16

CHAPTER

"JOSH!" OTIS EXCLAIMED. "Where in tarnation are you?"

"I can't tell you—I'm just calling." Josh was tempted to hang up.

"What do you mean, you can't tell me? Half a county's out looking for you, thinking you got killed in the storm. This sounds long distance."

"A little . . . I mean, I'm not saying."

"Are you okay?"

"I think so. My fingers hurt a lot and so do my ears."

"From the storm?"

"Yeah, sure was cold. Otis, I can't say no more. Can you call my parents and tell 'em I'm okay?"

"Why don't you call them yourself?"

"Because Dad'll get mad . . . say, Otis."

"What?"

"How is the owl doing?"

"Rough. She misses you feeding her."

"Do you think she'll ever fly again?"

"I don't know that she'll live yet. It all depends on

how stubborn she is. When you coming home, Josh?"

"Maybe never."

"Why—because of the cub?"

"Yup. If they let me keep him and quit letting bears get hunted, I'll come home."

"They won't do that, you know."

"Then I'm not coming home. But will you tell my parents I'm okay?"

"Josh, you know how your dad feels about me. Even if I called him, he won't believe me."

"Mom will."

"Maybe, maybe not. Is there any way I can contact you?"

"Nope."

"Will you call again, then, in case they let you keep the cub or something?"

"I'll try, but I'm not sure how. Say, Otis . . . if Dad doesn't believe you, just tell him I'm not Mookee Man."

"Mookee Man? What's that mean?"

"Dad'll know . . . just tell him. Okay?"

Suddenly the mechanical voice interrupted. "Three minutes are up. Please deposit a dollar twenty."

"I don't have no more. Good-bye, Otis."

"Josh."

"What?"

"Call me collect if you want. And one more thing . . . I sure am proud of you."

Josh hung up. What was there to be proud of? It

seemed like most of what he'd done had been pretty stupid. As he crossed the street to the grocery store, he looked at his hands. They were nearly black from feeding the fire. Josh spit several times in each hand and rubbed them together. Then he wiped his palms roughly on his jeans. His pants were so dirty the dark smudges barely showed.

When he entered the store, a voice surprised him. "Son, you'll have to leave your pack here at the counter."

Josh spun. A checkout lady stared oddly at him. The big woman had granny glasses with chains draping down each cheek. She watched his every move as if he had come to shoplift. Or could she have some other reason?

Josh nodded and dropped his pack where she pointed. Then he tried to ignore her, glancing around for a rest room. Near the rear of the small country store he found one used for both men and women. He slipped inside and locked the door. The mirror showed dirt and black grime smudging his face and neck. His hair looked like a straw pile. No wonder the lady looked funny at him.

Frantically Josh pulled paper towels from the dispenser and ran them under water. With a sloppy wad in his hand he started mopping his face. Soon the wad was filthy and his face looked hideous, smeared with dirt. Josh peeled off his shirt and splashed water straight from the faucet onto his arms and face. This worked better. After using most of the towels in the dispenser to dry himself, he tried to run his fingers through his matted hair. The tangled mop refused to be curried without a comb. Finally Josh gave up and dabbed at the globbed mess with a wet towel. It would have to do.

He looked cautiously around as he let himself out the door. He saw no one. Sighing, he started going up and down the aisles filling a grocery cart with food—stuff he could eat straight or fix camping. To the collection he added a ten-pound bag of dog food for Mud Flap and more milk and eggs for Pokey. Also about eight big boxes of farmer's matches. He could start a whole bonfire just with matches if he had to.

Ten minutes later he examined the pile of food he'd collected—it would give a pack mule a backache. But there was no telling when he could come back. Reluctantly he approached the fat lady with his cart.

The whole while she checked food, she kept eyeing him. "That will be thirty-six dollars and forty cents," she said.

Josh peeled crumpled bills from the dried wad in his pocket. Thirty-six dollars was nearly half of the money he had saved mowing lawns—money he'd saved to buy the new red ten-speed bike at Willy's Coast-to-Coast. Now he was wasting it on food.

Still the fat lady eyed him funny. "You camping?" she asked, watching him pack his backpack.

"Yeah," Josh said, trying not to look up.

"Where?"

"In Yellowstone—good-bye," Josh blurted, hastily gathering up his pack. He rushed from the store, not daring to look back. Only after reaching the cycle did he glance over his shoulder. In front of the store stood the woman, eyeing him. Josh breathed deep. An invisible hand was squeezing the breath from his chest. His head pounded like his heart was beating inside his skull. Did she know who he was? Why did she stare like that? He felt angry—why didn't she mind her own business?

Quickly he put the helmet on and strapped his pack to the cycle rack. He started the engine and drove straight ahead into town, past the lady. If he told her he was going camping in Yellowstone, he better make it look like that's where he was headed. After a few blocks he circled around through the side streets and headed back north.

CHAPTER 17
CHAPTER

BREWSTER DRUMMED his fingers deliberately on the dash of the patrol car. Already it was mid-afternoon. He stared up at the timbered slopes. Somewhere up there was a boy, a cub, and a dog—and Brewster feared the worst.

Since getting up yesterday, he'd mounted a massive search effort. Under orders from Scott Air Force Base, two Civil Air Patrol Cessna 180s were flying a grid matrix over the west slopes of the Bridgers. One of the planes was STOL-equipped to land in small mountain meadows if needed. Nearly fifty members of the volunteer Sheriff's Posse were combing the slopes on foot and horseback. A deputy had been assigned back at the station to answer phone calls and chase down leads coming in. His radio name, or handle, was Search-One.

Brewster keyed his walkie-talkie. "Sean, do you read me?" Sean O'Schanessy was somewhere up on the mountain directing the ground search. After a moment of silence, Brewster keyed the walkie-talkie again. "Sean, do you read me? Over."

"I hear you, lad," came the familiar crackle. "I'd

be pulling myself up a rock when you called to chat."

The sound of Sean's voice was comforting. "Have you found any sign yet?" Brewster asked, already knowing the answer. If they found anything, he'd be notified.

"No. The snow's gone. Unless the laddy made it through the blow, we'll not be seeing much. I have to tell you, I'm feeling funny on this one."

"Roger. Keep me posted." Brewster slumped forward against the steering wheel. Sean seldom expressed doubt. Was there any way a thirteen year old could have made it through the storm? In the valley, temperatures had dropped to twenty degrees. With wind chill, it reached well below zero. The storm had been violent. Brewster shook his head sadly.

Occasionally he heard the droning of search planes as they crisscrossed the sky. It was like looking for a mouse in a hay field. On the few occasions he had flown as a spotter, he'd discovered the patterns of nature. You didn't look for something individual. Instead you let your gaze sweep across the forests and meadows, looking for anything that broke the overall pattern—and it was a pattern easily broken. Tents, animals, rockfalls, garbage, broken trees, anything could interrupt nature's delicate tapestry.

Sometimes it seemed the planes repeated their paths unnecessarily. But Brewster knew that something hidden in the shadows of morning or noon sun might catch the eye in the dim wash of dusk. It was a huge game with a human life at stake.

Brewster picked up the mike from his police-band

radio and keyed it, flicking the selector switch over to channel six—the lone channel designated for search communication. This was the channel monitored by the young deputy at headquarters. "Search-One, this is Twenty-Two," Brewster said. "Have you heard anything?"

"Negative, Twenty-Two. I'll tell you what though. If that boy isn't found soon, we'll have every newspaper in the country here. This place is a zoo with people asking about the boy and his cub. Everyone's wanting to talk to you or other search members. Even animal-rights groups have called, wondering about the cub."

"What are you telling them?"

"I'm referring questions on the cub to the district Fish and Game headquarters. We might as well let them share the headache."

Brewster thought a moment. "Search-One, I'm heading over to the Fish and Game now. We should have some coordination with them or things could get sticky with the media."

"Roger, Twenty-Two. Keep me posted."

Brewster hung up the mike and slapped the dash hard with his hand. It wasn't bad enough having to coordinate a full-scale search. He also had to deal with family members, media, and the ever-present curiosity hounds. Add to this the sympathies of animal lovers in five states and this whole thing was getting absurd. He'd worked once on a rescue effort where a school bus slid into the Gallatin River. Fifteen children had died without as much attention and concern as this one boy and his cub were fetching.

Brewster backed his patrol car down the narrow logging road and turned around. Twenty minutes later he pulled into Fish and Game headquarters on the west end of town.

At the desk in the lobby, Brewster introduced himself to the receptionist. "Hi, I'm Deputy Bingham, Gallatin County Sheriff's Office. I'd like to speak with whoever's handling inquiries on the runaway McGuire boy."

"Oh, the boy with the cub?" said the young lady in her neat green and brown uniform.

Brewster nodded.

"That would be Deke Mizner—he's administrator for the district. Come this way." She led Brewster down a long, dark hallway and motioned into a drab office near the end.

Slid low in a chair, an overweight man squirmed upright and gave Brewster a doleful look. He made no effort to stand up or shake hands.

Brewster couldn't avoid staring at Deke Mizner. His bald head and humped shoulders gave him a mulish look. The man's appearance might have been overlooked had it not been for his stupid smile. A big triangular desk plate announced boldly the name *Mr. Mizner*. Even more conspicuous was the underlying title *Administrator*.

"Can I help you?" the man asked, sounding bored.

"Yes. I'm Deputy Bingham with the Gallatin County Sheriff's Office. I'm heading up the search for the missing boy, Josh McGuire. Have you—"

"Someone's not doing their job," Deke Mizner interrupted.

"I beg your pardon?"

Deke glared at Brewster. "All I've been doing for two days is answering calls for you."

Brewster acted surprised. "People are calling you about the McGuire boy?"

"No—about the cub," Deke said with a snort.

Brewster took the liberty to pull up a chair. "Why are they calling?"

"To ask if we're going to change the hunting laws to meet the boy's demands."

"Do they need changing?" Brewster asked innocently enough.

Deke splayed his fingers across his bald head. "I'm afraid that's our business, not theirs."

"Mr. Mizner, if you'll pardon my asking, why are bears hunted in the spring? Isn't their weight low? That's when they're trying to protect their newborn, isn't it?"

Deke Mizner settled in his chair. "Some have newborn—it's illegal to hunt them."

"I realize that," Brewster said. "But how do you tell when a bear is with cub? I've seen cubs wander hundreds of yards from their mothers."

"Oh, some get shot that way. But black bears aren't exactly an endangered species—they're scavengers."

Deke yawned. "If a few extra get harvested, we don't worry."

"Harvested? You talk like they're some kind of crop. Why even hunt them when they're low on weight and have rub marks in their fur?"

Deke's face tinted red with irritation, and he fidgeted with his pen. "Early on, their pelts are prime," he snapped.

"But they're sluggish and bold from craving food," Brewster said, pushing. "What kind of sport is that?" He riveted his gaze on Deke.

Deke spoke deliberately. "We're not changing a state law because of some runaway ... get that through your head," he said. "Now is there anything else, Deputy?"

Brewster saw beads of sweat surfacing on the man's forehead. Deke was a ladder climber, repeating rules and policy like a parrot. Brewster had seen his kind too often; afraid to make decisions unless it was by the book, coasting his way to a good retirement.

"Mr. Mizner, we've got newspapers as far south as Denver calling for information on this story. Whether we like it or not, that boy and his cub are getting attention. We'd best be able to justify everything we do or the media will chew us up and spit us out. They might do that anyway. What I stopped by for was to try and coordinate a common response."

"Response ... our response is no! It's your problem what happens to that spoiled kid. We don't go around changing state laws every time someone gets an itch. Another thing . . . the cub's not his. When you find it, the cub is to be confiscated. Is that clear?"

Brewster coughed. "There's concern what will happen to the cub."

"That's not your worry. We'll take care of its disposal. That's my jurisdiction."

"The same way you have jurisdiction over spring bear hunting, I suppose," Brewster said, standing to leave.

Deke glared up. "I don't know who you think you are, Deputy," he said. "But you take care of your job, and I'll take care of mine."

"We may not have jobs when this is over," Brewster said, walking from the office.

CHAPTER 18
CHAPTER

HALF AN HOUR after Josh hung up, Otis still chuckled to himself. Josh, the little rascal, he'd outfoxed them. His phone call was long distance. That meant he wasn't even in the Bridger Range. When this whole thing sorted itself out, there'd be hell to pay by someone. You didn't stir the soup this hard and skip supper.

Then he thought again of the boy's request. Josh was right about his father getting mad. Trouble was, Sam would get mad at whoever called. The more Otis thought on it, the less he cottoned to the notion. He'd call Bingham—let him do the talking. That's what officers were for.

When Otis tried calling Brewster at the sheriff's office, they transferred his call to some young upstart who said he was information coordinator for the search.

"I'm sorry," said the officer, "Deputy Bingham is not available. I can take any information on the missing boy."

"I've got information, son," Otis growled. "But if you want it, you have Bingham call me."

"What is your name and telephone number, sir?"

"Just tell him it's the guy who put him to work."

"What do you mean?" the young man protested.

Otis hung up. He walked to the backyard and stooped to look through the chicken wire at the wounded horned owl. In another week he could take off the splint and check the bone set. For now the owl was weak, and infection could still set in. Even without infection, sometimes animals just gave up. When that happened, they died as surely as if they were sick.

"You can't give up, old girl," Otis cooed. "There's a dumb-fool boy out there somewhere thinking of you. You better not disappoint him."

The phone rang and Otis ambled toward the house. "Hello," he answered.

"Hello, this is Deputy Bingham—you wanted to talk to me?"

"No, not really. But I figured I'd rather talk to you than Sam McGuire."

"What about?"

"Bingham . . . I just got a phone call from Josh."

"You what? Where is he?"

"He wouldn't say, but he asked that I call his parents and tell them he was okay. I figured you'd enjoy that chore."

"How was he? Is he coming home?"

"That depends. Have you met his demands?"

"Oh, for cripe's sake, you're not serious?"

"Josh is. I reckon that's what's important."

"Listen, are you going to be home?" Bingham asked.

"If you come out here, I'll put you to work."

"Over my dead body. I'll be right there."

Otis set down the phone and looked at the day's newspaper sitting on the kitchen table. Splashed across the front page was Josh's picture and the headline, SEARCH FOR BOY AND CUB CONTINUES. In a couple of days, Josh had the bureaucrats more excited than Otis had seen them in thirty years. Josh was sure enough a nervy little firecracker. But if he were older, he'd realize it was hopeless.

Otis looked out the window at the mountains. "Give 'em hell, son," he muttered under his breath.

Brewster Bingham set down the phone. How in blazes had the boy survived the storm and avoided search crews? Escaped prisoners from the local jail had been caught with less effort than this. Maybe Otis Sinclair was pulling a fast one. Before doing anything, Brewster wanted to talk to the recluse.

Ten minutes later, he pulled down the narrow twisting lane to the small cabin. Out back, Otis stooped over, working around his animal pens. Brewster walked up, skipping formalities. "Tell me everything the boy said, Mr. Sinclair. I want to know exactly when he called, what he sounded like, anything that caught your attention."

Otis spoke guardedly. "Like I told you, he didn't say much. Said he was scared to call home. His fingers and ears hurt, so he must have been caught in the storm. He said he wouldn't come home until his demands were met."

"How long did you speak to him?"

"Bingham, would you take that shovel and scoop some dirt around this chicken netting?" Otis pointed down at the bottom of the nearest pen.

Brewster stood his ground. "How long did you speak to him?" He let irritation grate his words.

Otis spoke sarcastically. "We talked exactly three minutes."

"Exactly?"

"That's when the voice came on asking for more money."

Brewster's thoughts scrambled. "How much did it ask for?"

Otis leveled a sharp stare. "I think it was a dollar twenty. Why? . . . don't believe me, huh?"

"No, that helps me narrow down how far away he was by telephone charge districts."

A fearful look stole into the biologist's eyes.

"Was he going to call back?" Brewster asked.

"Bingham, I think it's time you leave. The boy called in confidence, and I'm running at the mouth like a politician."

"Just tell me one more thing, Mr. Sinclair. Why should I believe you at all?"

Otis's eyes narrowed. "I don't care if you believe me or not. Josh wanted to get word to his parents, and I'm trying to do just that. Who cares if you find him? Fact is, I hope you don't. What Josh says is true; if the Fish and Game get that cub, it's dead meat.

And I never have liked their policy of spring bear hunting."

Brewster looked back as he turned to leave. "For whatever it's worth . . . I do believe you. Will you let me know if Josh calls again?"

Otis shook his head. "It's up to Josh. If he asks me not to, I won't."

"Do you realize you could be considered an accomplice?" Brewster added.

Anger gripped Otis's face and any tolerance disappeared from his voice. "Accomplice? . . . accomplice to what? I didn't know running away was a crime."

"It's a crime to impede a police investigation."

"Listen, Bingham. If you're going to threaten me like an idiot, then get off my property. Go ahead, get!"

Brewster regretted his words and tried to make amends. "Otis, let me back up a bit. I let my badge get bigger than my britches."

"That's pretty big," Otis said. "Why don't you see if they can both fit back in that patrol car of yours."

Brewster stared a moment, then shook his head and returned to his car. He'd pulled a dumb one. He saw the thin biologist staring at him as he crawled in and headed out the drive. Anybody else and he'd have arrested them for insubordination to an officer. But arresting Otis would be like spitting at a rattlesnake.

Brewster tried not to let thoughts of Otis bother him. Fifty men were on the mountain waiting, as well as two planes in the air. Now a big decision hinged on how much Brewster believed the old coot's words. Was Otis just trying to confuse the search?

As Brewster pulled onto the highway, he grabbed the walkie-talkie. It was time to trust his instincts and hope he wasn't playing into a bad hand. He might be too far out from the mountain to raise Sean, but he had to try. "Sean, this is Brewster. Do you read me? Over."

The radio crackled with static.

"Sean, this is Brewster. Do you read me? Over."

The reception was faint, but after a moment Sean's voice crackled weakly. "Aye. Where might you be? I'm barely hearing you."

"I'm heading back your way. I don't think the boy's up there."

"He'd not be up here, is that what you say?" Sean's voice sounded garbled and broken.

"That's right. We got a call from him. We think he's okay. Let me get closer to the mountain and I'll call you back." Brewster set down the walkie-talkie. Without meaning to he'd become genuinely concerned for the boy, and yes, dang it, the cub, too. Normally he stayed detached from people's problems. But somehow the two had gotten to him. Brewster picked up the police-band mike. "Dispatch, this is Twenty-Two. Patch me through to the McGuire residence."

"Roger, Twenty-Two. One moment."

Brewster heard the ringing, then a click. "Hello." It was Libby's voice.

Brewster took a deep breath. "Hello, Libby, this is Brewster Bingham. We might have something."

"Did you find Josh?"

"No, but Otis Sinclair got a call from him. He's all right."

Brewster heard Libby gasp. "You mean Josh called Otis and said he's okay?" she blurted.

"Yup, I'm going to—"

Suddenly Brewster heard a scuffle over the phone and Sam's voice broke in. "Officer, did you say Josh called Otis?"

"Yes."

"Why would he call him instead of us?"

"I'll explain, Mr. McGuire, when I get there. Be over soon."

"That bum's lying!" Sam shouted. "Josh would have called here first. I'm going over and end this foolishness."

Brewster heard a click.

CHAPTER 19
CHAPTER

"THAT CRAZY fool!" Brewster muttered under his breath. If Sam was drinking, he'd be a stick of dynamite. Especially with his son's life at stake. If nothing else, Sam struck Brewster as a man of his word—not much bluff.

He spun the patrol car around and headed again toward Otis's cabin. As he drove he contacted Search-One. They had a powerful base transmitter and could relay a message to Sean. "Search-One, this is Twenty-Two. Do you read?"

"Go ahead, Twenty-Two."

"I'm out of range. Can you contact Sean and have the searchers hold tight? Something's come up."

"Roger, Twenty-Two."

Brewster pulled up beside Otis's cabin. Sam McGuire hadn't shown up yet, but he'd be along soon—Brewster would bet on it. Seeing the yard empty, he headed for the cabin.

Otis met him before he knocked. "Come back to work, Bingham?"

"No. I called the McGuires. Sam wouldn't give me

a chance to explain. He's on his way over to settle with you."

"And you think I need you to baby-sit me?"

Brewster let his breath out slowly. Seldom did people push him to his limit, but this cynical recluse was testing the boundaries. "Otis, I'm here to help. If you don't like it, just say the word—I'll leave. You want to handle Sam by yourself?"

Otis glared.

"What's it going to be?" Brewster asked. "I've got better things to do than fight some hermit with a chip on his shoulder." As he spoke, Brewster heard a vehicle pull off the highway. He looked and saw Sam McGuire's green pickup racing up the drive. "Well, Otis? You want me gone?"

Otis glanced nervously toward the drive. His crusty voice seemed to melt. "Naw—you might as well stay for the fireworks."

The pickup slid to a stop beside the patrol car, and Sam jumped out. Slamming the door, he stormed across the yard. "What are you doing here, Officer?" he demanded.

"You didn't give me much chance to explain on the phone," Brewster said.

"Nothing much to explain if this liar is claiming Josh called him," Sam said, turning to Otis.

"He did . . . a couple hours ago," Otis said.

Sam's neck twitched and bulged with his temper. Whiskey shaded his breath and thickened his speech. "You're a lying sack of hog fat. He wouldn't call you."

It surprised Brewster how calm Otis remained. The

spindly professor stood six inches shorter than Sam and looked frail next to the tawny rancher. "He was afraid you'd get mad," Otis said. "Can't say as I blame him."

Sam turned to Brewster. "You're not going to believe him, are you? If Josh—"

"Sam," Otis interrupted. "When Josh called, I told him you wouldn't believe me. He said to tell you he wasn't Mookee Man. Said you'd understand."

Sam stopped as if hit by an electric fence. His gaze narrowed.

Otis pushed. "Sam, did you orphan that cub?"

"Did Josh tell you that?"

"If the cub was sleeping near the gut pile when Josh found it, I'd say it was orphaned."

"He's flat out lying."

Otis stood his ground. "Is he? I'm not sure Josh knows how to lie. Sam, if you don't pay the fiddler soon, he'll charge you double when he comes collecting."

Sam doubled his fists. "You're a damn liar, too," he spit.

"I don't think he is, Mr. McGuire," Brewster said calmly. "With your drinking, I'd say Josh has good enough reason to be afraid of you."

Sam spun around and headed for his pickup. "I don't need this!" he shouted. At the truck he stopped and looked back briefly. "I'll be back, Otis," he hollered, then jumped in. He fishtailed out the drive, spraying slush and gravel on Otis's old Ford Falcon and Brewster's patrol car.

Otis and Brewster stood quietly watching the green pickup disappear. They could hear its engine rev and whine wildly.

Otis spoke first. "Josh is a damn sight safer in the hills than with that maniac."

"What was all that about Mookee Man?"

The thin man shook his head. "I have no idea. It's some secret they have."

Brewster turned. "I need your help finding Josh."

The thin man shook his head stubbornly. "No . . . Josh doesn't need finding. He needs our help saving the cub. That's what started this whole thing—it's what's going to finish it. Sam, he's the problem."

Brewster bunched his lips in frustration but nodded reluctantly. "I suppose you're right—him and Deke Mizner."

"Deke Mizner?" Otis said surprised. "He brings animals out here from the Fish and Game—treats it like a joke. How's he involved?"

"He's looking to confiscate and dispose of the cub."

Otis snorted. "His idea of bear disposal is to stuff them and put an ashtray in their paws at some cheap motel."

Brewster nodded agreement. "I better run," he said. "There's still planes and search crews combing the Bridger Mountains. If Sam shows up, feel free to call."

Otis turned away without answering.

Once more Brewster headed out the drive onto the highway. He drove straight to the station. Things were happening fast, and he needed to move. Cars packed the normally vacant lot as he pulled in. What in the world was going on here? His question was answered as soon as he stepped inside. Reporters and camera people swarmed the lobby, asking questions of the dispatcher through her small window. Several turned and rushed up to Brewster. "Are you connected with the search?" they chorused.

Brewster raised his voice. "Ladies, gentlemen, we've had some new developments. In about a half hour I'll be holding a news briefing." Ignoring the shouting, he maneuvered past the reporters and let himself into the front office. Now was not the time for his favorite hobby: needling Beulah, the day dispatcher. She sat in front of the console like a parked Sherman tank. Her nasal voice sounded like a bullhorn.

Brewster spoke politely. "Beulah, please ask Captain Adams if I can meet with him in a couple of minutes. I need to call the search crews first."

Beulah nodded as Brewster headed for the radio room—command center for Search-One. The dingy eight-by-ten space doubled as staging for any search or rescue efforts. Search-One consisted of three different radios, two telephones, a computer, assorted maps covering all the walls, a desk, and temporary assignment for some unlucky soul. In this case a young deputy, Ed Green, manned the phones and chased down leads.

Ed Green spun around on his swivel chair as Brewster entered the room. "Brewster, am I glad to see you. We have several leads. Some guy over on the Boulder River saw—"

Brewster held up a hand. "Just a minute, Ed. I need to call Sean. Be right with you." He changed frequencies on the base transmitter and keyed the mike. "Sean, this is Brewster. Do you read?"

"I read you," came the familiar crackle. "What the devil is going on down there?"

"Otis got a call from the McGuire boy. We don't know where he is, but he's all right except for frost-bite."

"You think he's calling from some hunting cabin up here?"

"That's negative. His phone call was long distance."

Brewster heard a moment of silence. "Long distance, did you say?"

"That's right," Brewster answered.

"You mean we've been romping these woods for laughs? I'm getting to not like this child."

"Sean, until we find out more, bring your men off the mountain. Can you contact Civil Air Patrol and put them on hold?"

"Love to. Those buzz-boys have been flying over my head for two days now."

"See you when you get down."

"Brewster . . . if you find the child, I'm beholden if you'd let me strangle the little urchin."

Brewster smiled. "He's all yours. See you soon." He hung up and turned to the young deputy beside him. "What you got?"

"Four or five unconfirmed sightings. One from the Boulder River reported a boy that looked like Josh with two men in a pickup truck. One possible sighting near Judith Gap. Several calls locally think they saw the boy at these locations: the mall, the theater, and out near the dump. And a lady called from Gardiner. Said she saw a kid that looked like the one in the paper riding a motorcycle into Yellowstone."

Brewster shook his head and chuckled lightly. "A motorcycle, huh? All the leads sound pretty flimsy. You better chase 'em down though. Maybe something will turn up. Match the clothes Libby McGuire listed missing from Josh's room with the descriptions coming in—it might help. Another thing, find from the telephone company exactly what zone would charge a dollar twenty for the second three minutes of a pay-phone day call to Bozeman. I need the exact boundaries."

"Okay . . . oh, Brewster. About an hour ago, I got a call from AP News Network. They wanted a full update. I told them that their affiliates already knew more than we did—and cripe, they do. The buzzards know all about the dad's drinking and the older son's death—even about the dog. Unless the McGuires are flapping their lips, where are these pencil-boys getting all their stuff? It's sure not from us."

Brewster tilted his head back and ran his hands across his face. "You burp around these guys and they know what kind of pizza you ate. They monitor every transmission we make from this room. Let's watch what we say from now on . . . God, I hope we find that kid soon."

Beulah boomed loud over the intercom. "Brewster, are you going to keep the captain waiting all day?"

Brewster reached over and pushed the tab. "Be right there, Beeeulahhh." He massacred her name.

As he left he gave the young deputy a pat on the back. "Keep up the good work," he said. "I got a feeling this might get worse before it gets better."

Knocking, Brewster entered Captain Adams's office. He nodded to the square-jawed ex-marine. "Hello, Captain."

"Hello, Brewster." The stocky man looked up from his paperwork. "What've you got?"

"We think the boy's alive, but we're no closer to finding him. The media is crawling on us like flies. AP News called an hour ago." Brewster summed up the day's events. "The bottom line is," he said, finishing, "I don't think Sinclair's lying, but we can't count on him contacting us either if the boy calls again. Is there any way we can get a wiretap authorized for his house?"

The captain shook his head. "Not a prayer. Only the feds carry that kind of weight. What we can do is have the phone company hook up a pen-register. We have that authority."

Brewster thought. A pen-register recorded all numbers calling a particular telephone. Given a call, the phone company could then trace point of origin. He nodded to the captain. "It would help narrow down some of the leads anyway. An antisocial critter like Otis can't be getting too many long distance calls." Brewster stood. "Thanks," he said.

"Sorry I can't be more help."

Brewster nodded and headed for the door.

"One more thing," the captain said.

Brewster turned, his hand on the doorknob. "What?"

"Do what you have to, but watch your step. Everything we do is under the spotlight now."

"It has been since we started," Brewster said with a wan smile. He walked down the long hall toward the front office and the media. This was one side of search and rescue he actually feared. Reporters always made him feel like he was onstage and walking a gauntlet. He tucked his shirt in fresh and ran a comb through his thin hair. "Showtime," he said lamely to Beulah as he reached to open the lobby door.

The stout lady forced a cheeky, thin-lipped gesture, offering no encouragement.

A chorus of shouted questions echoed and greeted Brewster in the small lobby. He raised his hand and stood quietly until the group realized their shouting was futile. "Ladies and gentlemen," he said loudly over the remaining din. "A short while ago I called off the search for Josh McGuire in the Bridger Range. The boy phoned earlier today. He would not say where he was, but we do know his call was made long distance."

"Who did he call?" a loud voice shouted.

"All I'm free to tell you is Josh restated his original conditions, which you're aware of. He demands permission to keep the cub. He also demands that bear hunting be suspended in Montana."

"Why?" sounded several voices.

"He believes that confiscation of the cub will result in its death—a legitimate concern, I might add. He also fears other cubs might be orphaned, given present hunting laws."

"Is the Fish and Game cooperating?" called a shrill voice.

"Not at the district level," Brewster answered.

A number of voices murmured agreement. They had evidently tried contacting them.

"They won't even return our calls," one man shouted.

"My suggestion would be to contact the state office in Helena," Brewster said. "Let them know what response you're getting from the district." He held back a smile. "I'm sorry, ladies and gentlemen, that's all at this time."

Voices shouted behind him as he let himself back into the front office. He glanced at his watch. It was after six in the evening. His last meal had been breakfast.

Sam McGuire slammed on the brakes and came to a skidding stop in his yard. What a bunch of jerks! His boy was blaming him for something that was nobody's business. Libby had quit talking to him, her silence thick and accusing. The papers and TV were calling him an alleged alcoholic and saying he orphaned the cub. Now the fool deputy was choosing to believe that derelict, Otis. Josh was his son, not theirs, damn it!

Sam crawled out and spit at the gravel. He reached back and grabbed his bottle of whiskey off the seat, then headed away from the house toward the field.

Why didn't everybody just butt out of his life?

He trudged along, seething with anger and glaring at the bright sun creeping lower on the distant peaks. The jagged mountains looked ripped from the sky. He'd always loved the mountains. A warm breeze washed across his face. Out here in the field there were no moody wives, no Otis Sinclairs, no headlines, no accusing officers. Out here he could escape the unfairness of it all.

When he reached the middle of the sixty-acre parcel, he stopped. Standing alone, he swayed like a tree in the wind and raised the bottle to his lips. He sucked in a mouthful, rolling the sharp brew back and forth across his tongue. Then he held the bottle to the sun and watched the prisms of color flicker in the amber liquid. The hate, the bitterness, the sorrow caused his sway to worsen. Still he kept from swallowing the mouthful of liquor.

Suddenly with a deliberate grunt, he spit, belching the liquid out. The messy spray covered his pants and darkened the dirt at his feet. He tilted his head back. "Damn you!" he screamed at the top of his voice. "Where are you, Josh?"

He grabbed the bottle by the neck and flung it as hard as he could. When the spinning bottle struck the ground, it made a dull splintering sound. Sam collapsed to a sitting position on the rocky soil. He pulled his knees up tight in his arms. Tears welled in his eyes. "Where are you, Josh? Damn it, where are you?" he sobbed, his voice hoarse. "Please come home, Son. I know you're not Mookee Man."

CHAPTER 20

CHAPTER

HOLDING BACK the window shade, Libby had watched Sam pull in the driveway. She cringed as he stomped from the pickup. When would this nightmare end? But instead of coming inside, Sam headed for the open field west of the house. Libby sighed with relief and watched closer. What was he up to? He trudged along, a bottle swinging carelessly from his left hand. Then he stopped among the furrows, wavering.

Libby saw the bottle and shook her head. She felt her husband being wrenched from her, one bottle at a time. As if to confirm her thoughts, he took a sudden swig, then held the bottle up and stared at it. A moment later he gave it a terrific fling. What kind of demons was he battling? A wave of pity tugged at her—how badly she wanted to go to him.

Then she saw him slump to the ground and sit motionless. She waited for him to get up and come storming back—that was his pattern. But nearly a half hour passed, and finally she could hold back no longer. This was the father of her children. This was the man she promised to stay with for better or for worse. And if this wasn't for worse, nothing was! She headed out the door.

Moments later, Libby stepped in front of Sam. If he had seen her approach, he showed no sign. Hesitantly she reached down and touched his arm. Her touch might as well have been the wind. He sat motionless, bent over and brooding. Libby moved around behind him and began rubbing his back. Silently she kneaded and plied at his broad, powerful shoulders. Then gently she kneeled and slipped her arms around the front of his neck, embracing him.

She felt numb. Why did life threaten to take everything she had? Hadn't it taken enough already? Suddenly she felt Sam's rough touch on her arm. He squeezed. The grip brought her to tears, but not of pain.

"Libby, why do you still love me?" Sam blurted, his hoarse voice hollow and cracked. "How can you?"

Libby drew him tighter. "You're a good man, Sam McGuire. If you weren't, I wouldn't be here. Maybe it's because you loved Tye so much that everything's come unraveled. But that's not all your fault. Love's no crime."

A long silence settled between them. Not hateful silence, but rather a stillness touched by fear.

"Libby, what can I do?" Sam choked.

Libby held her answer a moment and weighed the words. "As long as I remember, Sam," she said, "you taught the boys to do what they knew was right— not to run from their problems. I came to you today because I saw you throw away the whiskey bottle. It wasn't empty, was it?"

Sam looked up briefly at the horizon. "No," he said quietly, returning his gaze to the ground. "No."

"Please tell me something, Sam. Did you orphan the cub?"

Sam would not reply.

Long shadows steeped the slopes as Josh bounced the cycle back into the meadow. His ride from Gardiner had been grueling with the heavy pack of food. He reached down and rubbed his right knee. Lower on the trail, he'd taken a spill. It didn't hurt the cycle, but he skinned his knee.

To save time, he drove as far up the slope toward the cave as he could and dropped off the pack. After coasting back into the gully, he covered the cycle with branches. All afternoon he'd worried about Mud Flap and Pokey. What if something had happened to them while he was gone? Was the bear still around—the one whose tracks he'd seen? He sprinted back and shouldered his pack, then scrambled up the slope toward the cave. Josh clenched his teeth. The sweat and rubbing of his pants made his knee burn as he climbed.

Finally, breathing hard, he caught sight of the two animals. They were curled together at the mouth of the cave, their legs overlapping. The echo of his footsteps caused Pokey to sit upright, wide eyed. Mud Flap looked up lazily and thumped her tail.

"Hi, guys! You okay?" Josh stopped to catch his breath, puffing hard. He held his side and ran to them. Both animals clambered up on him. "It's so good to see you," Josh panted. "Did you think I forgot you, huh? I brought you food." For several minutes he rolled and played with them, grimacing whenever his scraped knee was bumped. Soon the play became too rough, and he bowed out. They must be getting hungry.

After feeding them, Josh knelt and picked up kindling from his stack beside the fire pit. It looked like the fire was out, but Josh hoped for hot coals. If not, at least now he had matches. Scraping aside the top inch of ash, he blew, watching dull chunks of gray cinder glow magically. He laid a handful of kindling on the coals and kept blowing. Soon red-hot embers licked a new flame up through the tinder. Why wasn't Dad here to see how well this fire started?

While the animals ate, Josh fixed supper. He wrapped slices of Spam in tinfoil and let them sizzle on the coals. A can of corn simmered while Josh mixed pancake flour. He used a piece of slate for cooking. After downing every crumb, he stood and looked around. Darkness had covered the meadow and settled heavy on the trees. Josh stoked the fire, then yawned and glanced over at the sleeping animals. Mud Flap and Pokey must have tuckered each other out. They curled against each other, whimpering and shifting in their sleep.

Josh stretched out beside the fire and watched the stars. About eight zillion of them flickered and blinked like as many pinholes in a black ceiling. Falling stars streaked across the blackness, leaving long, thin tails like glowing slivers. Josh wondered if at home his mother or father was watching the sky and thinking about him—he was sure thinking about them.

Later, when the bright moon edged above the peaks, Josh left the campfire. He limped over and crawled around a jagged outcrop of boulders near the cave. Tucked under a large flat rock, he found a small patch of snow. The day's sun had melted the rest. Josh rubbed big handfuls of the cold wet slush on his skinned knee. Slowly the knee numbed, and the pain disappeared. He hobbled back to the fire and sat on a basketball-size rock.

Because he had plenty of matches, tonight he planned to let the fire die. He would, however, sit and feed it a while. Watching a fire was a good thing. Dad always said a fire's main purpose was companionship. Some of the biggest problems and deepest secrets got whispered into the flickering glow of a campfire. Dad said that a campfire understood a tad sight more than most people, and you shouldn't be ashamed to talk to one. So Josh started in, his voice sounding funny in the thin night air.

"You know what I want?" he said, letting his question hang a moment. "Well, I wish I still had all the money I'd saved for my bike. I wish my knee didn't hurt, and I hope they never find me and take Pokey away. I wish Tye hadn't died—I really wish that. I wish I was at home with everyone. I wish nobody had ever shot that owl at Otis's, and I hope someday it can fly again. More than anything else, I wish Dad and Mom still loved each other."

Josh doled another piece of wood onto the dwindling flames. "Guess that's too much to ask for, huh?"

The fire crackled in reply.

Crowding the flames, Josh listened to the wind moan across the slope. The cavernous overhang shielded him. But still he wore his jacket, hugging his knees and thoughts to his heart. Coyotes yipped and howled in the distance. Above the wind, Josh heard the eerie scream of a screech owl, followed immediately by the halted squeal of a rabbit. He knew the sounds for what they were: death in the night. He shuddered and moved closer to the fire.

When the faltering flames died to glowing embers, Josh stood stiffly and yawned. Did he dare let the fire go out? Even with extra matches, maybe another fire wouldn't start—fires were that way. But he had to let it go out. It had been risky, even now, allowing a flame through the evening. From high on a slope, a campfire could be seen for miles.

He hobbled farther under the ledge and rolled out his sleeping bag near Pokey and Mud Flap. They both awoke and moved over to lie on the bag. He curled one animal under each arm before falling asleep. He smiled to himself. Life wasn't so bad. In fact, at that instant, it was flat out wonderful and grand.

Once during the night, Josh awoke with a pressing pain on his forehead. After letting his senses keen, he realized Pokey was sitting on his head—upright, like a person on a stool. The cub yawned and rocked back and forth nonchalantly.

Josh pushed hard against the heavy burden. "Dang it, Pokey. Get off!"

The cub bounded off, acting greatly inconvenienced. Josh coaxed the cub back down by his side and cuddled the fuzzy mass under his arm. Soon the night drifted back into sleep.

It had been a short night. Over midnight coffee, Brewster dismissed Sean from search duty until the leads hardened. O'Schanessy's response had been, "You mean, my vacation, it's over?" Remembering the man's tired, hollow eyes, Brewster doubted the man knew what a vacation was.

Brewster sipped steaming coffee while he drove the half mile from his small house near the university. The June Montana air breathed crisp but not bitter. Hazy clouds filtered the dim wash of morning light, and Brewster yawned.

As he pulled into the station, he saw the captain's white Plymouth moored alone at the edge of the lot. A good thing about this time of morning was the quiet—morning shift had yet to arrive. Entering the front door, Brewster smiled at the weary duty officer, then headed for the radio room. He expected it to be empty but found the young deputy, Ed Green, with the phone glued to his ear.

"Here awful early, aren't you?" Brewster said.

The young officer smiled and set down the phone. "I think we got a break, but it doesn't make sense. The lady in Gardiner described a boy wearing tennis shoes, dirty blue jeans, a brown winter jacket, and a green flannel shirt. Now look at this." The deputy handed Brewster a piece of paper.

Brewster recognized the list Libby McGuire had

furnished them—clothes Josh might have taken with him. Every mentioned article was there. "But didn't that report have him riding a motorcycle into Yellowstone Park?" Brewster asked.

"That's what's got me. Where would he get a cycle, and how could he possibly hide inside the park with all the tourists around?"

"Did you figure out the phone boundaries?" Brewster asked.

"I was getting to that next—look at this." The young deputy stood and pointed at a large state map on the side wall. "That charge district extends from Big Sky, to Ennis, to about here, east of Butte." The deputy traced his finger in a big circle as he spoke. "From there it comes across north of Clyde Park and Wilsal, down to Springhill, and then south to Yellowstone."

Brewster pointed his pen at Gardiner. "The park boundary is the state line between Wyoming and Montana, right?"

The deputy nodded. "Gardiner is in that charge district. But something's screwy. The phone and clothes match, but hiding in Yellowstone and riding a cycle don't figure."

"Have you asked the McGuires if Josh had a cycle?" Brewster asked.

"No. I was just calling them when you walked in."

Brewster picked up the phone. "Let me call them," he said. "I need to check how Libby is doing anyway."

Shortly he heard Libby's voice. "Hello," she said.

"Libby, this is Brewster Bingham. Sorry to be calling this early. Can you tell me, does Josh own a motorcycle?"

"No. Why? What have you got?"

"Did he have access to a cycle?"

"Well, Tye had a dirtbike before he died. But that's been stored down in the toolshed ever since."

"Is it still there?"

"Yes. I'm sure it is . . . I mean, we haven't noticed it gone. Just a second. Let me wake Sam and ask him."

Brewster heard muffled talk in the background. Soon Libby came back on. "Sam says he saw it there just yesterday."

"Okay, thanks. If you think of any way he would have a cycle, let us know. It's just a lead we're chasing down."

"I will," she said. "Thanks for calling."

"Libby."

"What?"

"How you doing?"

Brewster heard a hesitation, then, "I'm okay."

"Well, don't be afraid to call."

"I won't."

Brewster hung up the phone slowly. "Scratch that," he said. "He doesn't have a cycle, unless he stole one. Why hasn't anyone seen him? It's like he evaporated. If he was hauling a cub and a dog around Yellowstone Park on a motorcycle, we'd have our phones ringing off the hooks. And yet, the clothes can't be a coincidence. What are we missing?"

The young deputy shook his head. "He's outfoxing us."

"And I'm getting tired of it," Brewster said.

CHAPTER 21

CHAPTER

"DID THEY spot Josh on a motorcycle?" Sam asked with a grumble, shifting upright in bed.

Libby set down the phone. "No," she said. "They're just chasing down leads. Someone must have reported a boy on a cycle. I suppose everyone and their sister calls in with something odd they've seen."

Sam wanted to get mad at Libby. He didn't know what for, but somehow she seemed to blame. She was in such control—like she knew something but wasn't telling him. He hadn't answered her yesterday when she asked if he orphaned the cub, but he could tell by her voice she figured he was guilty. So what if he was? He sure hadn't killed a mother bear on purpose. "What are you staring at?" he snapped, seeing Libby watch him.

"Nothing. I'm just trying to figure out where Josh could have gotten a cycle."

"Oh, for Pete's sake. You don't think he could carry a dog and a bear on a motorcycle, do you?"

"Just wondering," Libby said. "Are you sure you saw the cycle in the shed?"

"Yes, I'm sure I saw the cycle in the shed," Sam mimicked. "You think I'm lying?"

"No, I just . . ."

"You just what?"

Libby did not reply.

Sam smirked as he dressed. Shortly he pulled on his jacket and walked from the house. A person couldn't even get sleep around here. What a joke— didn't anyone have a lick of common sense? No wonder they hadn't found Josh yet, chasing down goofball leads like that motorcycle. Sam headed to the barn and started fixing rotted boards on a stall. After yanking and cussing at several stubborn ends, he crossed over to the toolshed for a crowbar.

On his way out of the shed, crowbar in hand, Sam glanced at the covered motorcycle. It was still there. He couldn't exactly see it with the tarp hanging all the way to the ground, but it was under there. Sam took a couple more steps toward the door and looked back. He felt foolish. Of course it was under there— he was starting to think funny like everyone else. And still he stared at the shape formed by the dirty green canvas. Something seemed odd.

"Oh for Pete's sake," he muttered under his breath and walked over to the tarp. He yanked up a corner and stared.

"Son-of-a . . . that little jerk!" Sam hissed, his words biting the air. He felt his face flush hotly. Braced boards held up the oily canvas. He slammed the crowbar downward, splintering two of the boards. "Smart aleck! You think I'm a fool," he roared.

Sam trembled with anger. Libby probably helped Josh take the cycle. The two were probably laughing right now at how dumb he was. Sam stormed up to the house. He was tired of being made the fool.

"Libby!" he shouted, kicking open the front door.

"What?" she called.

"What?" he parroted. "You know what. You knew the cycle was gone, didn't you?"

Libby rushed in from the kitchen. "The cycle . . . gone? Whatever are you talking about?"

Sam glared at her, trying to catch her in the lie. She acted so serious and concerned. Oh, but she was good. "Did you know he took the cycle?" he shouted.

"The motorcycle? How could he have . . . ?" She covered her mouth.

"Don't tell me you didn't know anything," Sam said. Having told the officer that he'd seen the cycle yesterday in the shed, now they would say he was lying if they found out it was gone. It was Libby and Josh who were lying. They had put the braced boards under the tarp. "You knew the cycle was gone," Sam said, pointing his finger at Libby.

She grabbed his arm. "Sam, quit it! Think—how could I? I never get out to the toolshed."

He shrugged away her hand and picked up the telephone and dialed. As he waited, he muttered to himself.

"Search and Rescue. Can I help you?" came a young voice.

"Let me talk to Officer Bingham," Sam stated.

"One moment."

Soon Brewster came on.

"Is this Officer Bingham?" Sam demanded.

"Yes. Who is this?"

"This is Sam. Josh took Tye's motorcycle."

"Are you sure?"

"It's gone. What more you want?"

"Okay. Can you describe the cycle?"

"It's a red Honda Enduro 125. Tye worked two years to earn money for it."

"Did Josh know how to ride it?"

"I suppose Tye let him on it a time or two. But there's no way he could've headed out in the middle of the night carrying a dog and a bear."

Officer Bingham's voice was deliberate. "It looks like Josh has done a lot of things we didn't think he could."

Sam cussed and slammed down the phone.

Libby sat with her elbows on the kitchen table. She cradled her forehead in the palms of her hands. "What did he say?" she asked weakly.

Sam glared at her. "Everybody's acting like Josh is their son," he muttered and headed for the bedroom.

After hearing Sam's sharp cussing and the click, Brewster waited a moment. Then he hung up and turned to the young deputy. "We're on to something, Ed. Get a description of that cycle spotted in Gardiner. Oh, another thing. Find out if she actually saw the cycle going into Yellowstone . . . or if he was just headed that way."

Within minutes the deputy set down the phone. "Brewster, she only saw him headed that way. She had no idea what make the cycle was, but said it was red, and the kind that kids ride down through the ditches and climb hills with."

"A dirtbike."

The deputy nodded.

"Bingo!" Brewster slapped the table and turned to the map. "That boy has had us on the wrong trail from the start. If I were his father, I'd be proud of him." Brewster puzzled at the map, his finger wavering over Yellowstone. Suddenly he turned. "No! Josh is too smart to head into the park with all the people. If he came into Gardiner, he's in the area. But where is he hiding? Listen . . . are we sure he's out camping? What if he's hiding at someone's place?"

The deputy shook his head. "The lady at the store said he was filthy, smelled like smoke, and bought the kind of foods you cook on a campfire."

"Then he'd almost have to be somewhere in here." Brewster pointed to the southern end of the Gallatin mountain range. "It's a big area, but no bigger than the Bridgers."

The deputy nodded.

Brewster threw his pen down. "Okay, let's run with it."

"Hold it a second." The captain's gravelly voice sounded behind them in the doorway.

"Good morning, Captain," said Brewster, turning to greet the unsmiling man.

The captain walked in. "We'll see how good it is. Look at this." He threw a fresh copy of *USA Today* on the bench.

Brewster looked down and whistled softly. Splashed across the top of the front page was Josh's picture and in bold print the heading: A NATION HOLDS ITS BREATH FOR YOUNG BOY AND CUB IN MOUNTAINS OF MONTANA.

The captain growled, "Today we've got crews showing up from every major network. Notify the boy's parents so they're prepared. Starting now, I want every press release across my desk first. By God, if I'm going to get hung over this thing, I want to be the one stringing the rope."

Brewster hurriedly explained the morning's discoveries. He pointed at the map and voiced his thoughts.

"Hope you're right," said the captain. "This thing's got a short fuse. I want you to push, push hard. Check with the telephone company on the pen-register every hour. I'll assign an unmarked police car to stake out Sinclair's residence in case he makes contact with the boy."

"How about the media?"

"They all want to be part of this party," said the captain, "but not a one wants to help hold the cake. You let me take care of them. Just find that boy!"

"Captain," Brewster said.

"Yes."

"I about half agree with why the boy ran away. So far, the Fish and Game have washed their hands of this. Can we make them answer to the media?"

The captain nodded. "You bet."

Brewster thought of Deke Mizner and smiled.

Brisk air woke Josh before the sun had fully risen. He rubbed sleep from his eyes with the back of his fists and scrambled from the bag. His mouth tasted awful—Dad called this moose breath. Josh winced when he bent his stiff knee.

Everything was so different up here. At home Mom often scolded him for not finishing the food on his plate. Here his hunger never went away. At home he fussed and fretted over any old scrape or cut. Now he was learning to ignore pain. What he could not ignore were his feelings. Any time of day, tears were only the next thought away.

And often that thought was of Dad. It just wasn't fair, Josh thought. He remembered when he used to argue with Tye over who Dad liked best—they even asked Dad once. Without hesitation Dad had replied, "I love you both the same. You're like my two legs. One's no better or worse. I couldn't get by without either of you."

Maybe that had been true, Josh thought. Because now Tye was dead, and his father wasn't doing so good. It was like Dad had lost one leg, and now he was mad at the other leg for everything that went wrong.

Josh looked out across the mountains. Morning

streaked the sky, and mist flooded the lower meadow. Today he had a lot of chores. If bad weather set in again, he needed a good supply of firewood and kindling. He could also make up some stick bread. That's what Tye and Dad had called it when they mixed pancake dough real thick, then wrapped it around a stick to cook like a hot dog.

Josh looked over at Pokey. He wanted badly to unleash the cub, but he'd run away. Every time something scared Pokey, he bolted. Suddenly Josh hit on an idea. He undid the leash from the rock and tied the end around Mud Flap's neck. With rope between them, the animals could run and chase each other. Josh had only to call Mud Flap to retrieve the cub.

Feeling good about the new arrangement, he set off down the hill for a load of firewood. "Mud Flap, you stay," Josh ordered. The command was unnecessary. The animals were chasing each other excitedly around camp, ducking and feinting.

Fifteen minutes later, Josh returned with branches heaped high in his arms. He couldn't see the animals. "Hey, Mud Flap, Pokey, where are you?" he hollered. Quickly he dropped the wood and looked around. Inside the cave, the cub and dog had quit playing and were busy eating and tearing at something. Josh ran in and gasped.

Scattered everywhere was food from the backpack. Pancake flour covered everything, including Pokey. He looked like a four-legged ghost. The jerky and candy bars were devoured. Four crushed cans of tomato soup stained the white blanket of flour. All the cookies were gone, as well as the eggs for Pokey's mixture. The powdered milk and oatmeal were broken open and mixed with dirt.

For an instant Josh could not move or talk. It was like he'd been hit. Then he grabbed the leash and dragged both animals roughly away from the feast.

"Quit it!" he screamed.

They struggled to return, clawing and pulling. Together their small legs nearly dragged Josh back into the cave.

"Mud Flap, no!" Josh yelled, kicking at the dog's rump. He missed and fell but caught Mud Flap's attention. She sulked up, tail between her legs. The cub hadn't given up. He bawled and grunted with desire. Spinning his rump toward the food, he tried to reach a hind leg toward a chunk of candy bar.

Josh stood and dragged the struggling cub out in the open. After tying both animals, Josh walked back to the backpack. There he slumped to the ground and started to cry.

CHAPTER 22
CHAPTER

JOSH'S TEARS made tiny craters in the white pancake flour. Why was everything going wrong? Didn't Pokey and Mud Flap know they had just eaten or wrecked most of the food?

Slowly he sifted and picked through the cluttered mess. It angered him. Mud Flap hadn't touched her dog food. And that was all that was left. Josh made up his mind. Now for sure he had to find more food. Frustrated, he left Pokey and Mud Flap tied up and headed alone toward the ridge with his fishing line.

When he topped the notched saddle between the peaks, he stared at the lake. A tent and fire still marked the distant shoreline. "Aren't you ever leaving?" Josh muttered. Would they leave if he crawled up on their camp during the night and made funny sounds? Maybe he could pull out their tent stakes. He'd never do it, but wouldn't it be fun to let Pokey go inside their tent? Hunger gnawed at Josh's stomach as he headed back.

When he entered camp he'd made up his mind on one thing. No matter what it tasted like, he could get by for a while eating Mud Flap's dog food. If it didn't kill a dog, it wouldn't kill him. Hesitantly he started chewing the crunchy nuggets. They tasted awful, and even with water they clumped and stuck in his mouth. How in the world could a dog get excited about this?

After several handfuls, Josh spit out what was left in his mouth. The taste made him want to throw up, and he came up with a new idea real quick. He untied Mud Flap and grabbed Pokey's leash. Then he made an announcement. "C'mon everyone. Let's go bean a grouse. I saw some in the meadow yesterday."

Josh remembered how Tye used to chuck rocks at grouse. The dumb birds just sat there while rocks whizzed by. With a little luck, Tye usually hit one. Josh snugged the leash over his wrist and set off down the hill. "I never beaned nothing before," he admitted to the dog and cub. "But if Tye could do it, so can I."

As they hiked toward the meadow, Josh started filling his pockets with good beaning rocks—anything about the size of eggs. He chucked several at a tree. The rocks were okay, but not his aim. He missed by several yards. If he couldn't even hit a tree, would he ever hit a grouse? Why couldn't he throw as good as Tye? These questions haunted Josh.

He trailed Pokey and Mud Flap around the big meadow looking for clumps of shrubs or trees. Tye had taught him that grouse liked to hang out in thick underbrush.

The first grouse flew up with a flutter from within ten feet of where they walked. Josh watched it power its way to a nearby branch like an egg beater. He tied Pokey to a stump and told Mud Flap to stay. Then ever so slowly he crouched and moved toward the gray bird. Twenty feet away, he stopped and started throwing.

The bird, about the size of a small chicken, sat motionless while rocks whistled past. Finally one rock hit the branch it sat on, sending the grouse into a sudden burst of flight. Josh watched the bird drum its wings down across the meadow and out of sight. "I'll get you next time," he vowed under his breath.

He wondered if there was any harm in beaning grouse. Otis explained to him once how animals depend on each other. He said each critter fits into a big puzzle—he called it a life cycle, or chain, or something. If you kill one animal, sometimes you hurt another. Josh wasn't sure if grouse were part of anything like that—he hoped not. He just wanted to bean one for supper.

After returning to get Pokey and Mud Flap, Josh headed straight across the meadow toward the far side. On the upslope the sagebrush grew like thicket. He wasn't even sure he could chuck stones very good in the stuff, but he'd try. Still two hundred feet off, he saw several grouse burst up from a big patch of trees. Also a deer bounded out as if scared. When the doe came to a stop up the slope, she looked back down into the thick undergrowth.

"The grouse must have scared her," Josh guessed, talking aloud. "Maybe there's more grouse still in there. Come on, let's go." He headed out at a trot, towing the cub. When they approached the tree line, Pokey started balking on the leash. Mud Flap growled low.

"Quit it, girl. You'll scare the grouse," Josh said. He snubbed Pokey's leash to an aspen tree, then turned. "Mud Flap, lie down. Lie down and stay."

Reluctantly the border collie obeyed, still uttering short murmuring growls. Josh shook his head and headed for the thicket. He moved slowly. Several times he walked within a couple feet of grouse before they flew up. The gray birds were nearly impossible to spot.

Off to his left Josh heard a crunching sound. Probably another deer. Then he heard Mud Flap growling behind him. "Mud Flap, shut up!" he hissed over his shoulder. How could he ever sneak up on grouse with a dog growling for the whole world to hear? But still the dumb mutt kept growling, and then she barked. "I'm going to kill you," Josh muttered, heading back toward the dog.

Now Mud Flap's barks mixed with snarls. Ahead and to the left, branches started breaking. Something big was moving forward toward the meadow. What could it possibly be?—maybe a person? A deer would have run away at the barking. Or could it be . . . Josh grew weak at the thought.

The crunching sound quit. Whatever it was had entered the grassy meadow. Mud Flap's bark pitched high with urgency. Josh had never heard her like this. He broke into a run. When he stumbled into the open, he caught sight of a huge black bear hurling toward Pokey. "It's a bear! It's a bear!" Josh screamed, standing helpless.

Pokey bawled and raced side to side on his leash. He bit frantically at the rope, his little marble eyes boiling with fear. And then, mouth wide, the monstrous animal hit him. On the run, it snatched Pokey by his thick hair, shaking him. Without slowing, the bear hurdled to the end of the leash. The rope snapped tight, ripping Pokey from the bear's powerful jaws. Instantly the bear spun and charged again. Long stringy slobber whipped back from its parted lips.

Pokey was on his feet and running, his bawls pitched ragged with fear. He scrambled away from the charging bear but somersaulted as he hit the end of the leash.

"Don't kill him!" Josh shrieked, horror strangling his words.

A sudden streak of black and white flashed from the side. It leaped directly at the bear's face. The bear roared and grunted with surprise.

"Mud Flap—get him, girl!"

The bear spun, flailing at the ducking and twisting dog. Several times Mud Flap yelped, but she kept up her attack. For the moment, the little dog befuddled and angered the bear. Like a pesky gnat she spun, lightning fast, nipping and diving at the wild creature's face. At home, Mud Flap could jump five feet in the air to catch a Frisbee. But this was no Frisbee. The bruin exploded with savage grunts and snorts, lashing back.

Josh dashed directly toward the tree where he'd tied the cub. His path brought him within ten feet of the fearsome fight. Beside the tree, he fell to his knees and jerked at the rope. It was useless—the struggling cub had pulled the knot hard. Josh grabbed for his pocketknife and fumbled it open. Hands shaking, he hacked at the leash.

An ear-splitting bellow made him glance up. Mud Flap had snapped and bit hard on the bear's nose. The huge beast reared high, arcing Mud Flap up through the air. Coming down, Mud Flap let go and hit the ground with a grunt. She scrambled clear, then attacked again. Once more the bear bellowed and slobbered, lashing out.

The fight moved closer to Josh. With a final slash the rope snapped. The cub burst free and bounded across the meadow. He bawled and frantically pumped his small front feet back under his rump to escape.

Josh ran after the cub—he'd better stay with Pokey. Not until they started climbing toward the cave could Josh catch up and grab the trailing leash. His gasps for air stung his chest. Pokey breathed with heavy rasps also, eyes wild.

Josh looked back and could see Mud Flap still ducking and snapping in a circle around the huge black bear. The bruin stood in one spot, swiping powerfully at its little attacker. "Come here, Mud Flap. Come here," Josh yelled. If Mud Flap quit attacking, maybe the bear would go away. "No!" Josh screamed. "Quit it, girl!"

Mud Flap looked up at Josh for a split second. In that moment a thundering paw caught the little dog across the chest. A dull thud sent her spinning through the air. She hit the ground and rolled, then lay still. The bear roared fiercely and raked the ground, advancing toward Mud Flap.

"No!" Josh screeched, letting go of Pokey. He grabbed a big stick on a dead run and headed down the slope. With a long, curdling banshee cry, he slipped and scrambled across the meadow, swinging the stick in circles over his head.

Hearing the scream, the bear paused and watched Josh's wild advance. It stood its ground. Finally, with Josh barely a hundred yards off and fast approaching, the bruin suddenly turned and loped away toward the lower valley.

Josh stumbled up to the downed dog and fell to his knees. Mud Flap breathed raggedly; her little black-and-white body was matted with blood. Several long gashes peeled back the skin along one shoulder. Cuts crisscrossed her nose, and one leg bent wrong under her body.

"Mud Flap!" Josh wailed, tears swelling in his eyes.

The dog tried to rise, then collapsed in the grass with a weak yelp. Josh looked around frantically. Up the slope he saw Pokey racing out of sight over the lip of the cave.

Mud Flap whimpered lightly.

Arms shaking, Josh cradled the little dog's bloodied face against his cheek. "I'm going to help you, girl.

Don't die. I'm going to help you," he sobbed. "You dumb, dumb dog!"

Tears mixed with blood and smeared Mud Flap's muzzle. She whimpered in reply.

But even as Josh repeated his words, he had no notion what to do.

CHAPTER 23

CHAPTER

JOSH CRADLED Mud Flap's head, sobbing wildly and pleading aloud, "Don't die, Mud Flap . . . please don't die!"

Her eyes blinked weakly.

Josh knew Mud Flap was very near death. There was something in her stillness. He had seen it on the ranch with sick horses and weak calves. The stillness could not be seen so much as felt. Something had to be done quickly. But what?

Otis might help, but the nearest phone was in Gardiner—or was it? Hadn't there been a small cabin before he reached the highway on his way into town—the one with electricity and the big propane tank outside? Maybe the place had a phone. Whatever he did, he couldn't just sit here like a crybaby.

"Mud Flap, I'll be right back," Josh sniffled. He laid her limp head gently in the grass. Mud Flap's slow, halted breathing had a raggedness to it. She no longer opened her eyes. Josh stood and ran toward the cave.

A red sun burned low like a big ball of fire over

the peaks. In a couple of hours it would be dark—why couldn't things ever go wrong in the morning? Approaching the cave, Josh found the cub near the woodpile, cowering against the rolled-up sleeping bag. The leash trailed loosely in the dirt. Pokey's plum nose hung low. He had a wild look in his tiny button eyes.

"Pokey. Come here, boy. I've got to tie you up."

The cub quivered.

Josh started forward, but the cub curled its lips and blew menacingly. Suddenly it swatted the ground, uttering a breathy "woooff!" The cub's crazed look held a challenge. Josh backed off and reached in his pack, pulling out a handful of dog food. "I won't hurt you. Here, boy . . . you'll like this," he said quietly.

The cub glared. Then a mournful cry leaked from its throat. On hands and knees, Josh crept forward, holding out the dog food. Hesitantly Pokey nosed it, his legs quivering. Then surprisingly, he crowded past the food and clung to Josh's leg. Within seconds, Pokey worked free a front paw and started nooking and sucking the pad. Josh bent forward and hugged the cub.

Now, as never before, Josh needed to stay and show Pokey the world wasn't all horrible and lonely. But he couldn't stay, and Pokey would never understand why. Josh pushed the cub away and picked up the leash, his eyes watering. "I'm sorry, Pokey. Don't be scared. I've got to go help Mud Flap. She's hurt!"

As he wrapped the leash around the big rock, Pokey tugged against the rope. Then the cub sulked, his fuzzy chin drooped nearly to the ground.

"I'll hurry, I promise," Josh said, doling out dog food on the ground. Pokey was probably still full from his midday feast. Josh glanced over at the dwindling fire. A flame might keep the big bear away, so he heaped on some wood.

Across the meadow, Mud Flap's black-and-white body showed as a clump in the shaggy green grass. Josh slipped on his jacket and sprinted frantically down the hill toward the cycle. This was taking too long, but what else could he do? He had to get the dog to Otis.

With his hands shaking, Josh made sure he had the choke pulled out and the gas turned on. Then he switched the key and leaped on the kick starter. Each time the engine faltered, he felt hollow terror. Tears were starting to blur the numbers on the speedometer. He blinked, leaping again and again.

Coughing smoke, the cycle finally sputtered, then roared to life. Josh raced the engine, knowing Tye said not to—but there wasn't time to let it warm up slow. He spun up out of the ravine, swerving wildly over to Mud Flap.

The little dog appeared dead. A breeze ruffled the hair on her bushy tail. Josh stared, holding his breath. Finally he saw the slight movement of Mud Flap's chest. He exhaled. "Atta girl. Don't give up."

The cycle idled roughly, popping and echoing like

a sharp drumbeat. Josh was about to pick up the dog when he noticed the hard bottom and sides of the milk crate. Quickly he peeled off his thick brown coat and stuffed it in for padding. Mud Flap whimpered and moaned as Josh lifted her into the cramped box. Her body twisted awkwardly in the small space, leaving her head flopped over the edge.

Breathing hard, Josh mounted the cycle and flipped up the kickstand. Then he gunned the engine and barreled off toward the lower meadow, spitting leaves and twigs out behind. The sun balanced on the ridge and cast a deep golden red reflection. Long shadows hid much of the trail.

Every bump flopped the small dog's head around, and she yelped weakly. The sound tore at Josh, and he glanced back desperately. Maybe he shouldn't have ridden down like this—it might kill Mud Flap. Reluctantly he slowed and kept picking his way down the trail, speeding up for short distances, then braking again.

Halfway down, Josh's white-knuckled grip on the handlebars caused his arms and shoulders to sting and cramp. The sharp pain burned in his muscles like a knife blade twisting in circles. How must Mud Flap feel?

Josh bunched his lips and kept riding intently. The trail curled and bent downward. At one point the path appeared strange and new. Had he taken a wrong turn? For several long minutes he rode, fearful and bothered by the thought. Then a brief splash of dusk light showed a trace of tire mark on the path. He sighed. It was a track left from his ride into Gardiner.

After leaving the rutted trail, the gravel road seemed like an interstate. In minutes Josh pulled up beside the brown log cabin. He hesitated. There were no cars. Shadows from the roof reached across the yard, which was blanketed in pine needles. Except for two robins working the ditch for worms, nothing moved. Soon it would be dark. The electric power line caught his eye. It ran from a pole near the road into the cabin. A small separate wire had been strung below this. Josh took an excited breath. At home, that was for the telephone.

He shut the engine off and set the kickstand. Gently he felt Mud Flap's side. A faint heartbeat pulsed, but her breaths were shallow and halting. Josh ran up to the cabin and tried the door. He twisted at the locked knob, then ran around the side and tried a window. No luck. Frustrated, he went to the next. After prying at each opening, be grabbed a branch. Standing to the side of the rear window, he swung the makeshift club forcefully. The glass shattered, and Josh reached in past the jagged ends to undo the catch. Everything he was doing was wrong. But what other choice did he have?

After crawling inside, Josh glanced about. The small two-room cabin was fancy. In the rear was a kitchen and bathroom. The front room was a living room with a nice couch. In fact, the furnishings were better than anything at home. The living room was even carpeted. Judging by how clean everything was,

Josh guessed the cabin was used often. A TV and stereo lined one wall. Alone on an end table sat a yellow telephone. With his hands shaking, Josh ran over and picked it up. The most beautiful dial tone he'd ever heard buzzed in his ear.

He couldn't remember Otis's number. Nor did he know how to call collect—so he dialed the operator.

"Hello," said a woman's voice.

"Hello. I want to talk to Otis Sinclair."

"In what city?"

"Bozeman," Josh said, exasperated. Where did she think he lived?

"What is your billing?"

Josh panicked. "My billing? What do you mean?"

"How do you want this call charged?"

"Charged? I, ah . . . Otis, Otis said he'd pay."

"So you want this collect?"

"Yeah."

"And what's your name?"

Josh tried to keep his voice calm. "Why do you need to know my name?" he asked.

"It's required for collect calls. Your name please?"

"Josh," he blurted. "And, ma'am . . . let the phone ring a long time. Otis doesn't like answering telephones."

Surprisingly fast, Otis came on the line and accepted the collect call. His gruff "Hello" was like music. Josh's words boiled out. "Otis, this is Josh. Please help me? Please, you've got to help me."

"Now hold your horses," Otis said. "Are you all right?"

"Yeah, but Mud Flap's hurt, and you have to help her."

"Where are you?"

"Otis, a big bear tried to kill Pokey, and Mud Flap saved him. But the bear hurt Mud Flap. Please help me—please." Josh knew his voice was quivering and he was almost screaming, but he couldn't help it.

"Okay, okay," Otis said. "But Josh, you have to settle down. Tell me real slowly—where are you?"

"I'm in a little cabin. Can you come right away? Mud Flap's hurt and—"

"Josh!" Otis growled sharply. "Listen! I'll help you, but calm down. Tell me exactly where you are. Okay?"

Josh took a deep breath. His palms were wet, and he felt chilled to the bone. When he tried to speak slowly, he couldn't control his stuttering. "O-o-o-kay. I'm just below the campground up Rock Creek."

"You mean, in Paradise Valley?"

"Yeah. There's a li-ittle cabin I broke the window on."

"Is that the cabin on the south side of the gorge?"

"Yeah."

"Okay, Josh, I've been by it. How bad is Mud Flap hurt?"

"R-r-real bad. She has lots of cuts, real bad ones. A-a-and her leg is bent funny."

"Is she alert?"

"S-s-she won't open her eyes. Please hurry—she's dying."

"Okay, listen carefully. I'm a long ways away. Get

a blanket over her and press lightly on any place that bleeds. I'll leave right away."

"B-b-but Otis, I can't stay here. Can't I just leave Mud Flap, and you pick her up?"

"No! If you want to save her life, you stay with her."

"You won't tell anybody, w-w-will you?"

"No, but keep Mud Flap warm and don't leave her."

Josh heard a click and then buzzing. Now the dial tone sounded menacing—it left him all alone again. He trembled. Soon it would be dark. What if Otis got lost? Maybe he'd call Dad or the police right away. Thoughts of his dad's anger made the trembling worse.

Quickly he ran over to the front door and unlocked it. In minutes he had Mud Flap laid in a crumpled pile on the living room carpet. He tried to position her comfortably. Then he pulled his jacket over her bloodied and limp body. Little trickles of blood oozed from her open gashes. Josh pulled off his shirt and bunched it gently against the wounds.

Goose bumps peppered his bare arms and chest as he waited. He looked around the small cabin. Glass covered the floor where he broke the window. Josh felt in his pocket for the small wad of remaining bills. He ought to leave twenty dollars on the table to pay for the window. Then he'd have barely thirty dollars left from his bicycle money.

Josh looked down at the carpet. Smeared bloodstains surrounded the dog. Josh wiped at one of the marks with his hand, only smearing it worse. Why hadn't he carried Mud Flap to the kitchen's tiled floor? He didn't have enough to pay for a new carpet—for sure that would make him Mookee Man. His mom and dad would never love him again. He couldn't control his shivering and he had to gasp for air with short, fast breaths. Was it the cold, or was he scared? Maybe Mookee Man shivered when he was evil and bad.

Josh spotted a blanket on the couch. Quickly he got up and grabbed it and wrapped it roughly around his shoulders. Huddled over Mud Flap, Josh stared at the matted blood on the little dog's chest. He waited anxiously for each faint breath.

"Captain!" Brewster shouted. "Something's happening."

Captain Adams rushed from his office. "What's up?"

"Otis Sinclair is on the move. Fifty-Five is tailing him east over Bozeman Pass. I called the telephone company. The pen-register showed a long distance call about thirty minutes ago to his place. Came from somewhere north of Gardiner. The phone company is tracing it right now."

"Okay, let's move. Fifty-Five—is that Kelly?"

Brewster nodded.

The captain shook his head. "I'd sure feel better, Brewster, if it was you in that car instead of a young rookie. Oh well, listen—tell Kelly to keep his distance. I don't want to spook Sinclair if he's headed for the boy. And I don't want names used over the radio. Those camera boys are like sharks on blood right now."

"Some have started following the patrol cars, Captain."

The stocky ex-marine tightened a fist. "If any of them trail a squad car, write 'em up. Announce that over the radio for their pilfering ears."

Brewster pursed his lips and frowned. "Captain . . . this evening the boy's story aired on every news network in the country. What the devil do you think is going to happen now?"

A look of bitter frustration crossed the captain's chiseled face. "If we don't find him by morning," he said, "the media will hang us. Call the Search and Rescue. Have as many men as possible ready for a night search."

"A night search? But Captain—"

"We have no choice. As soon as we hear from the telephone company, I want things rolling. Wherever the search crew heads to, Brewster, I want you with them. Tonight we might be making decisions on the run. I need you in the field."

"Are we to confiscate the cub if we find it?"

The captain nodded. "We have no choice. By the way, do you know Deke Mizner?"

"I wish I didn't," Brewster said. "Why?"

"The jerk called about an hour ago from the Fish and Game. He read me the riot act. This morning he issued a statement to the media—accused us of sitting on our butts. He must have reminded me a dozen times he was district administrator."

Brewster's face grew hot. "Sitting on our butts?" he grumbled. "I'm surprised Deke can stand without a crane."

The captain forced a weak smile. "I'm getting real tired of sitting at the bottom of this fire drill."

The intercom buzzer grated the air, followed by the dispatcher's nasal voice. "Captain, a call on line four."

"Beulah, get their name. I'll call 'em back."

The dispatcher came back insistently. "But Captain, it's the governor."

CHAPTER 24

CHAPTER

OTIS SINCLAIR pressed hard through the canyon, shadowing the Yellowstone River south. At last he cleared the steep ravine and squinted over at the dim, moon-polished river. It stole away into the darkness like a silver phantom highway.

As he drove, thoughts ate at his mind. Earlier, the news networks, ABC, NBC, and CBS, had all carried Josh's story. They made him out to be a local hero. Hogwash—he was a scared thirteen year old with a drunk father, not unlike thousands of other kids. Still Otis couldn't deny a touch of jealousy, and yes, respect and fondness.

Otis glanced in his rearview mirror. The highway had little traffic. One set of lights had followed him since Bozeman—probably someone headed home to Gardiner or to one of the ranches. He snapped on the dome light and checked his watch—a little past ten. An hour had passed since Josh had called.

Before leaving, Otis had contacted a veterinarian friend that he'd worked with in Bozeman. Not mentioning the details, he told the vet to be ready in three hours to do midnight surgery on a wounded dog. There were closer vets, but if this pooch was as chewed up as it sounded, Otis wouldn't trust her to just anyone.

Soon the reflecting sign for Tom Miner Basin gleamed green in the dark. Otis slowed and swung onto gravel road. If memory served him right, the road for Rock Creek branched to the right within the next half mile. From there it climbed three or four miles to the cabin. How in blazes had Josh gotten down here? No wonder they hadn't found him.

Lights flickered in his rearview mirror, and Otis saw them turn and follow him off the main highway. Surely no one was following him tonight. It was probably one of the full-time residents who lived up the Tom Miner road. As he drove, though, he kept glancing at the mirror.

Once more the lights flickered, and Otis stopped and glanced back. He swore softly to himself. A boy was waiting with a dying dog, and here he sat, stopped. Was he getting paranoid in his old age? When the lights failed to reappear, Otis headed out again. At night it was hard to tell—the lights must have been on the lower road before the turnoff. Continuing up, the rutted narrow road remained dark.

Deputy Kelly maneuvered his unmarked patrol car cautiously up the base of Rock Creek. He had no intention of letting Sinclair get out of sight. On the other hand, he could not follow him up the canyon without being seen. Until the moon was higher in the sky, the night was too dark to drive without lights. He also remembered Brewster's warning not to alarm

Sinclair. Seeing the taillights slow, Kelly reluctantly stopped and snapped his lights off. He called in on his radio while he watched the bright dots start forward again. They flickered and bobbed up the canyon like twin fireflies.

"Dispatch, this is Fifty-Five," he said.

"Go ahead, Fifty-Five."

"I have subject in sight, headed up Rock Creek. I cannot, repeat cannot, pursue without exposing myself. Please advise."

After a long wait, Brewster's voice broke in. "Hold your position, Fifty-Five. You're in a box canyon. Set up a roadblock and detain subject when he comes down. Notify me at that time. Do you copy?"

"Roger. Do I have jurisdiction in this county?"

"Don't you worry about that. I'll get you authority."

"Ten-four." Deputy Kelly set down the microphone and cracked open his window. The cool evening air felt good against his face. Cautiously he backed up and repositioned his car. Even with the moon up, he'd be out of sight until Sinclair rounded the bend. Sinclair would be a sitting duck.

After Brewster set down the handset from talking to Deputy Kelly, he walked back over beside the captain. Together they huddled around the map taped high on the radio-room wall.

"Okay, Captain," said Brewster. "The telephone company said the call to Sinclair came collect from a small cabin located about four miles up Rock Creek." Brewster traced his finger roughly along the map, squinting. "That would have him about . . . here," he said, poking his finger bluntly against the map.

The captain nodded, then glanced at his watch. "Ten-thirty. Is the search crew ready?"

"Should be," Brewster said. "We borrowed a bus from the detention center to haul the men. We'll have the rescue van along for any medical emergencies. If we're still looking in the morning, we'll bring up some horses and put planes in the air. One more thing—Libby McGuire should be here in a little bit with an unwashed piece of Josh's clothing. The men with the hounds need it for scent."

The captain sat down wearily and toyed with a pencil on the desk, flipping it end over end. Brewster knew something was eating at the man. Ever since talking to the governor, he'd been in a bad mood. Whatever got said was one-sided. All Brewster heard was a lot of "yes, sirs."

"Anything else you want, Captain, before we head out?" Brewster asked.

"Yeah. Let's keep this under wraps. We don't need family and press second-guessing us tonight. Keep in touch with me by telephone or radio relay. You'll have extra deputies along, so keep a roadblock down at the Tom Miner cutoff to Rock Creek."

"Why there, sir?"

"To keep out news hounds."

Already Brewster had his coat in hand. Pausing at the door, he turned back. "Excuse me. If you don't mind my asking, what did the governor have to say?"

Continuing to flip his pencil, the captain looked down at the desk when he spoke. His voice was deliberate, almost reminiscent. "I guess the governor's catching hell. Animal-rights groups and news organizations are demanding to know what he's doing about the boy and the cub."

"What can he do, Captain?"

"Plenty. Evidently Deke Mizner shot his mouth off a bit too much. The governor's instructed the Fish and Game boys to shut him up. When the dust settles, he's going to personally review Mizner's statements to the media and his refusal to cooperate with us."

"I don't understand, sir. Why is the governor getting involved? We're doing everything we can."

"He figures bad publicity will hurt the state's tourism industry and the out-of-state hunting dollars. Add to that lawsuits filed by animal-rights groups . . . cripe, we're talking lots of money and bad publicity. Might have something to do with his reelection next year, too. Bad national media exposure for a politician can be a stick of dynamite."

"Why did he call you?" Brewster asked.

"He told me to get off my duff and find the boy," the captain said, slamming his fist on the counter. "What exactly does he think I've been doing?"

Brewster set his chin stubbornly. "Okay, then, let's find him. Sir, will you be staying here at the station?"

The captain nodded.

"Okay, I'll stay in touch." Brewster turned and headed out the door.

CHAPTER 25

CHAPTER

WHEN OTIS first saw the small cabin, it looked deserted, blanketed in darkness. A motorcycle flashed into sight as Otis swerved in the short drive. Had he misunderstood Josh?

"Josh," Otis hollered, climbing stiffly from the car.

A cracked and frightened voice echoed from inside the darkened structure. "Otis! Otis! I'm in here. I was scared you weren't coming."

"Hi, Josh. How's Mud Flap?" Otis shouted back.

"Not so good, but she's still breathing. What took you so long?"

"Seventy miles," Otis said, entering the cabin. In one hand he carried a small first-aid satchel. He groped for the light switch. With a snap, a bright glow flooded the room. Otis stared in disbelief. Huddled on the floor sat Josh, hair matted and face covered with dirt and blood. His eyes were hollow and scared, and he cowered under a blanket, teeth chattering. Next to him was a jacket-covered mound.

Josh's tired, expectant look was haunting. "Did you tell anybody?" he asked.

Otis saw stark fear in the boy's eyes. "Nope," he replied.

"You sure?"

"I'm sure; now let's take a look at your pooch." Otis knelt down and pulled back the coat. He let out a long whistle. "Looks like she took on a threshing machine."

Josh remained silent.

Otis moved deftly. He pulled open his bag and slipped a thermometer under the dog's tail. Carefully he lowered his head to her chest and listened. Then he thumbed open an eye.

"Will she be all right?" Josh pleaded.

Otis pressed a finger against the dog's gums, then withdrew it. Next he reached his finger in and probed the back of her throat. "I don't know," he said quietly. "She's lost a lot of blood and she's in shock." Pulling the thermometer out, he held it to the light. "Ninety-six degrees. Should be at least a hundred and one. Josh, get me a little piece of kindling wood from the fireplace. Something about eight inches long and big around as a broomstick."

With the blanket still wrapped around his shoulders, Josh obediently did as he was told. Otis laid out Mud Flap's badly twisted leg and gingerly taped the wood on as a splint. Then he grabbed Josh's coat and tossed it to him. "Here, put your jacket on. I'll need that blanket for the dog."

"She won't die, will she?" Josh asked. "You've saved lots of animals."

"Only those that wanted to live," Otis answered.

"It'll all depend on Mud Flap. Here, take that blanket and spread it on the front seat. We have to hurry." He draped the first-aid satchel over his shoulder and scooped Mud Flap into his arms.

"Just a second," Josh exclaimed. He jumped up and ran over to the table. Rummaging in his pocket, he pulled out a crumpled twenty-dollar bill and laid it down. "I kinda wrecked the place," he said, returning to pick up the blanket.

Otis smiled softly and followed Josh out the door. "Josh," he asked, as he laid the limp dog onto the seat, "how did you get here?"

"On that motorcycle," Josh said, pointing to the machine hulking in the dark. "It belonged to Tye."

Otis shook his head and wrapped the dog carefully in the blanket. Then he looked at the shivering boy. "Until we get her to the vet, there's not much to do except keep her warm. You're coming with me, aren't you?"

"No," Josh blurted. "I can't leave Pokey."

Otis stared hard at the bedraggled and frightened boy. "Josh, you're in no condition to stay up here," he said. "Your mom is worried sick. And all hell has broken loose at home."

"It has up here, too," Josh mumbled weakly.

"Will you go get Pokey if I come back in the morning?"

Josh moved warily away from Otis, his eyes guarded. "I'm not ever going to let them take Pokey," he said. With that he ran toward the cycle and jumped on.

"Hey, Josh . . . wait!" Otis yelled. It was no use. Josh had the cycle started and fishtailed it out of the yard. Otis rubbed his hands over his face and groaned. Didn't the fool boy know when to quit?

Remembering the dog, Otis hurried back to his car. Everything had become muddled. Here he was trying to get Josh to come home and at the same time hoping against all hope they wouldn't catch him. He thought Josh foolhardy and had told him as much. And yet, Josh had sure stirred up the hornet's nest.

Otis careened down the narrow gravel road as fast as he dared, resting a hand on the dog to keep her from jostling off the seat. He felt a fragile but stubborn pulse of life. Why was it some animals fought so hard to live while others gave up in a blink?

Otis had forgotten all about the lights he'd sighted coming up. Nearing the bottom, he swerved around a sharp right turn. One second his lights played into moon-softened darkness. The next, bright beams leaped back from the night and blinded him. He jammed on his brakes, swerving back and forth in a dusty stop. His car rested only feet from a dark-colored sedan. "What the devil?" he muttered.

A booming loudspeaker split the night, echoing, "Mr. Sinclair. Step from your car and put your hands on the hood."

Shaking with fear and anger, Otis opened the door and stepped hesitantly into the bright lights. He shielded his eyes with one hand.

"Hands on the hood," came the bellowing voice.

Otis placed his hands cautiously on the car and

looked over his shoulder. He half expected to see a ten-foot tall giant emerge. Instead a young officer with a slight build stepped from the dark sedan and walked up behind. The man appeared anxious and scared. He started frisking Otis.

"For cripe's sake, do you mind telling me what this is all about?" Otis demanded.

"I have orders to stop you."

"Bingham put you up to this?"

The officer showed faint surprise and motioned with his hand. "Would you please step back to my car?"

Otis stood his ground. "No! I've got more important things to do," he said, pointing toward his own car. "There's a dying dog in there. If she doesn't get help, it'll be your neck—big time!"

Muscles twitched in the officer's cheeks. He shined his flashlight through the window, exposing the motionless bundle on the front seat. "Where did that come from?" he asked nervously, wiping a sleeve across his forehead.

Otis took a step toward the officer, causing the man to tense. "You listen to me," Otis said. "Get Bingham on the radio. If you don't, you'll be mopping floors at a burger stand for a living."

"Are you threatening me?" the young man challenged, running the tip of his tongue across his thin lips.

"No, I'm making you a promise. If that dog dies, you'll wish you'd never met me."

The officer studied Otis, then turned abruptly. "I

need to call Deputy Bingham anyway." He ushered Otis back to the patrol car.

Shortly Brewster came on the radio. "Is subject alone?" he asked.

"Yes, sir . . . ah, except for a dog."

"A dog? What the—"

Otis reached and grabbed the mike. "Bingham, is that you?" he interrupted.

"The one and only," came Brewster's husky voice. "Care to tell me what you're doing down there this time of night?"

"I haven't time to explain, Bingham. I'll tell you this much. I have the boy's dog. The little mutt's been tore up terrible. If she doesn't get to a vet quick, she's dead—might be anyway. You tell this greenhorn of yours to let me by or the dog's death will be your fault. I reckon as how the newsboys would have a heyday with that, wouldn't they?"

The radio crackled, then Brewster's terse voice broke in. "Fifty-Five, does he have a wounded dog with him?"

The young officer reached over and grabbed the mike back roughly. "He appears to, sir."

Again there was a long pause. "Fifty-Five. We're on the move here. Escort Mr. Sinclair to the veterinary clinic. Stay with him until we notify you. Is that clear?"

Otis smiled smugly. "Looks like I have me a baby-sitter."

The young officer's face reddened visibly in the reflection of the headlights. "Ten-four," he snapped into the mike. He hung up and turned to Otis. "Where we headed?"

"I'm headed for Doc Chambers on North Seventh. You head anywhere you like."

"Follow me," ordered the officer, failing to hide his irritation.

Otis opened his car door. "Officer," he said, "your car's facin' the wrong direction."

CHAPTER 26

CHAPTER

JOSH RODE hard in the darkness, his headlight bobbing. Why had Otis asked him to go get Pokey—so they could kill him? He rode even faster. Ledges and rocks blurred past. His speed sent him flying off the trail several times, bouncing him roughly out across gopher holes and sagebrush.

Halfway up to the meadow, he entered a small clearing. His aching arms needed rest. Josh slowed to a stop. The whole valley was visible from the middle of this clearing—one of the few places not surrounded by trees. A half-pie moon rose higher in the sky, blanketing the ground with an eerie glow. On the valley floor, the main highway paralleled the river. Closer, but less visible, Josh recognized the faint outline of the road branching in to Tom Miner Basin. He breathed deeply and stretched.

Suddenly, a set of lights emerged from the bottom of Rock Creek—that would be Otis. Then another set blinked into view close behind. The cars followed each other out. An empty feeling of betrayal choked Josh, and he swallowed again and again to hold back his tears. On a night like this, nobody would be up Rock Creek except Otis, and he'd said he hadn't told anyone. Josh watched in disbelief. The cars trailed onto the Tom Miner road, then crept toward the main highway headed north.

Hot tears filled Josh's eyes. Above the drumming engine, he shouted, "Otis, you fink! . . . you big, lousy rat fink!" The night swallowed his words. Josh felt empty, and he sat alone on the mountain—more alone than he'd ever been in his life.

Slowly he filled with anger, and then hate. It made him a wild thing. He twisted his resentment into the throttle and barreled upward into the darkened woods. Otis had looked him right in the eye and sworn he'd come alone. The liar! The liar! Josh's stomach churned. He spun and careened around the sharp turns, coming dangerously close to spilling.

As the trail wrenched and bounced beneath him, Josh's thoughts boiled. Now they would come looking for him. They would take Pokey away and kill him. Probably Mud Flap would die, too. And when his dad got hold of him—Josh didn't dare think about that.

The solution came to him simply—there was really no other choice. He'd load up Pokey and ride around Buffalo Horn Peak, past Ram's Horn Lake, and down Porcupine Creek. The trail would drop him out on the other side of the mountain range near the state border. From there he would ride away into the night. He'd go to Idaho, or maybe Wyoming—someplace where they didn't kill cubs. It occurred to him he'd never see his parents again. The thought left him numb and cold and bitter.

Again he thought of Otis and spit savagely at the night. Otis had been his friend—one of the few. Josh rode hard into a burning tunnel of anger. No longer was there a sky or trees or sound. All he could see was the bending, gut-wrenching path. All he could feel was the aching betrayal.

A thin mist hazed the air, fuzzing the stars out of focus. Ahead the trail crested a sharp butte, disappearing into the night. Josh kicked to a lower gear and cranked full-out on the throttle. The cycle leaped forward and screamed up and over the ridge into the blackness. In the split second as the cycle left the ground, Josh realized his error—the narrow trail dropped steeply away and hairpinned to the right.

Everything slowed. Floating smoothly, Josh felt the cycle standing up in midair. The headlight swept its luminous beam across the misty dark sky. The engine revved into a tinny, piercing whine. Then a sudden jar knocked everything back to full speed. Josh bucked forward over the handlebars. An invisible fist slammed into his chest and left arm. A bone cracked loudly. Branches snapped and splintered. Glass broke. Metal smashed. Then everything became dark and still.

As they prepared for the search, Brewster got the call from Deputy Kelly about Otis and the hurt dog. A short while later, on his way from the station, he met Libby. She seemed distraught.

"Brewster. This is all I could find," she said, holding out an old pair of boots. "He's wearing his tennis shoes. The day after we found him missing, I washed all his clothes and cleaned his room. I did it to stay busy, but I suppose that was pretty silly, huh?"

Brewster shook his head. "Not at all, it's okay. These will do just fine."

He took the boots over and handed them to the search crew. Two men held hounds tethered on short leashes.

Libby looked at the dogs apprehensively. "What's happening?" she asked.

Remembering the captain's order to keep things under wraps, Brewster tried to sound casual. "We're just following up another lead. I'll call you in the morning if we find anything."

Libby turned to leave, but then looked back with a haunted, helpless look. "Brewster," she said. "I don't know how long I can stay at the house."

"Are things getting bad?" he asked.

Her quivering chin said more than words. "The longer this goes on, the worse Sam gets," Libby said. "This afternoon he threatened two reporters with a rifle."

"Do you want me to have him arrested?" Brewster asked.

Libby's eyes opened wide like a frightened doe. At the same time her lips hardened in a thin line. "No—not that, not yet," she said. "I'm scared for Josh, though . . . if we ever find him."

"We will," Brewster said, handing Libby the captain's phone number. "No matter when, don't be afraid to call him or come in here, okay? The captain's staying at the station tonight."

Libby nodded and rushed to her car.

Brewster shook his head as he watched her leave. She was so helpless. He whistled to Sean, who stood talking to several of the searchers. "Let's go," he hollered.

Leaving town, Brewster checked his watch—nearly eleven. The sky was dark and salted with stars. To the west, heat lightning flickered on the horizon. O'Schanessy relaxed on the seat next to Brewster. As they drove into the night, they discussed maps and trails and planned their strategy. If the boy had ridden to the cabin on the cycle, they would try to follow his tracks by flashlight. If and when the boy went on foot, they would track him with hounds.

After they finished their planning, they drove without speaking. Brewster stared numbly at the road and let a dozen mile markers flick past before he spoke again. "Sean, sometimes I wonder why we're looking for the boy. Is it so he can go home and get the holy tar beat out of him by his father? Or so the governor can get reelected, and the media people can get their scoop?"

"I'd be looking because it's my job," Sean answered. "And because young boys should not be alone, or cold, or scared on a night like this."

They continued into the night in uneasy silence.

———

Josh tried to breathe but could not. A huge hand gripped his chest, pressing him toward the darkness. Against the fear and pressure, Josh gasped. A thousand needles jabbed his lungs and floated him away from his thoughts—he was suffocating. He gulped frantically. The maddening pain teased him with air—it dared him to punish himself. Josh lay on his back, grimacing with each breath. His legs twisted to the right. He could not feel his left arm. And until he breathed more air, he feared to move.

The wind had picked up, and Josh's thoughts drifted with the mountain breeze. Was this how Pokey's mom felt after she was shot? Josh tried to scream for his own mother but could barely move his lips.

This was just like that dumb rabbit, Josh thought. On a hunting trip, he and Tye had seen a rabbit scamper from the woods, followed closely by a bounding bobcat. The closer the cat drew, the more frantic became the chase. Feeling the bobcat's hot pursuit, the rabbit looked back in desperation. At that instant it ran headlong into a tree—the chase was over.

Josh knew he'd done the same thing.

Overhead the stars blurred and moved side to side. Somewhere in the night a coyote yipped, its broken cry sounding hollow and distant. Slowly Josh risked deeper breaths. He tensed and moved his right arm. Then he moved each leg. The right leg moved hard, making his thigh burn. He reached down and felt oozing wetness. His left arm was doing something crazy. He tried to move it and realized it was lying awkwardly under his back. Josh rolled over. A pain knifed through his fist and shoulder. His gut knotted and he threw up. Then a cloud of black, darker than any night, poured into his head.

Josh breathed into the middle of the pain, waiting for it to fade. Then he grimaced and tried to move his left arm. Instant, hollow sharpness bit at his shoulder, and the thick blackness washed over him again. Clutching at the burning in his thigh, Josh struggled to his knees. His jacket was open in front, and one sleeve was nearly ripped off. His bare chest was sore, and he cradled his arm gingerly. A thick knob protruded from the skin of his forearm. Touching it made bright colors swarm through his head. He nearly fell over.

He looked around in the pale moonlight. The cycle rested silently, upside down like a mangled ghost. On the sloped bank, a tree, nearly six inches across, stood splintered in half. Josh felt sick again. He started to sweat and nearly fainted. Awkwardly he stood and climbed back up to the trail. His thoughts muddled, and he shook his head trying to clear his brain. Slowly it came to him: he'd wrecked the cycle, Otis was a fink, and now they knew where he was. What would Dad say? Suddenly the night grew colder.

Josh stumbled up the trail. How was Pokey? And how close was the cave? Hadn't he ridden a long time before crashing? Every movement of his left arm caused Josh to cry out. He hugged it to his side and continued. What would Tye have said if he could see the twisted heap of metal that used to be his shiny new Honda?

Josh found he could concentrate on only one thing at a time, and so he worried about Pokey. What happened to little cubs if they died? Didn't anyone make a grave, and get flowers, and pray for them like when Tye got killed? Josh's legs grew heavy. Saving an animal's life could sure be a lot of trouble, he thought, as he trudged into the dark.

After only a hundred yards, he entered the big meadow. He was still a long way from the cave, but he could see the familiar darkened slope across the clearing. Tears of relief broke over his cheeks. He tried to rush forward but could not—each step had become a painful, deliberate thing. Twice he tripped and fell to his knees, crying silently.

Josh heard a trickling sound drawing closer in the dark. He continued forward and concentrated on the sound until it rose near his feet. The whispering water blended with the breeze. He bit at his pain and dropped to his knees. The stream flowed within arm's reach. Several times he attempted to scoop at it with his right hand, but he lacked the strength to cup his fingers tightly. With a painful grunt, Josh fell forward on his chest. Flames burned in his arm, and he lay trembling.

Finally he rolled to his side and let his face drag into the icy water. The numbing fluid filled his mouth and he gulped at it. If the stream had been deeper, he could have rolled completely in. Icy fingers would have numbed away all his pain and worry and anger.

Coughing and choking, Josh drank his fill, then struggled back to his feet. The world seemed to tilt and swirl. Awkwardly he gazed up at the hillside and at the darkened hollow. Was Pokey okay?

For the next hour Josh battled the pain, the darkness, and his feelings. When at last he topped the lip of the cave, his strength melted away. He felt dizzy and had to force the last few steps. Again his mouth tasted like he'd chewed on chalk, and his voice cracked horribly when he tried to speak. "Pokey, are you there?" he croaked. "Pokey?"

The cub scrambled from the shadow of the big stone. Despite his pain, Josh stooped and rubbed the familiar fuzzy bundle. "I got myself in a mess this time, Pokey," he grunted.

The cub whimpered and nosed at Josh's legs, tugging at the leash. Josh hobbled around, rolling out his sleeping bag. Desperately he wanted to escape the pain. Everything hurt. His chest and head ached, and his thigh felt numb. Every time he breathed, his left arm and shoulder throbbed.

When he crawled in the bag, he left Pokey tied up—close enough to cuddle. No longer could he sit up. Even thinking had become an impossible chore. He breathed a labored sigh, letting his thoughts drift and evaporate.

Barely had he fallen asleep when the pain jerked him back awake. It was like someone trying to drag him from the bag with a knife. Vaguely Josh was aware of Pokey crawling into the bag beside him. Josh relaxed, feeling the warmth.

CHAPTER 27
CHAPTER

OTIS DROVE with one hand on Mud Flap's shuddering ribs. He could feel her struggling for life. Why was it so important to come back to a world that didn't care? Otis knew he'd never put up this much of a fight.

Soon the highway dropped off the pass and curved down toward the Gallatin Valley and Bozeman. It irked Otis having to trail behind Deputy Kelly. The officer insisted on leading the way, going exactly the speed limit. With a droll smile, Otis pushed harder on the gas pedal. Downhill, he swiftly passed the officer's car. He stared straight ahead, pretending he was alone in the night. Deputy Kelly remained behind, and Otis chuckled.

Approaching North Seventh Avenue, Otis saw lights on at the animal clinic. Judging by the mangled mass on the seat, his old friend, Doc Chambers, would have his hands full. Doc greeted him in the parking lot. The man was balding and plump, with a rock-solid robust belly. His powerful shoulders and meaty fingers did little to promote a professional image. Close behind them Deputy Kelly pulled in and stepped from his car.

"What's with the escort?" Doc asked curiously, seeing the deputy.

"I'll explain later," Otis said. "Just ignore him."

The vet nodded. "Okay. What've we got?"

"The dog's been attacked by a bear," Otis said, carrying the bloody bundle inside.

Doc Chambers raised an eyebrow but asked no further questions.

Deputy Kelly followed them in, his wide leather belt creaking as he adjusted it. "Mr. Sinclair," he said. "Now I'd like you to come with me down to the station."

Doc Chambers looked up. "Excuse me, but I'll be needing Otis for the operation." He turned and winked at Otis.

The deputy looked irritated and befuddled, as if trying to regain a control he'd never had. "My orders were to stay with you," he said to Otis.

"Then be a good baby-sitter," Otis said, "and either hold my hand or wait out front."

Deputy Kelly spun angrily and stomped into the waiting room. Immediately, Otis and Doc went to work. Having helped operate on Fish and Game animals, Otis needed no instructions. He laid a heating pad over the dog. Next he grabbed a hair clipper and delicately started shaving around every gash.

The quiet vet had already given the dog a shot of anesthetic and was hanging up an IV bottle with a plasma drip. "She's shocky," he said quietly, "so I went light on her dose. She's going to need every ounce of strength to stay with us."

Otis nodded, always amazed at how the man's big sausage fingers worked so deftly. While Otis cleaned the cuts, Doc began setting the leg.

"I think she's got a couple broken ribs," Doc said. "But we don't dare operate on her in this condition. If she lives, we'll take X rays in the morning. We may have to let the ribs heal on their own."

Soon a wrapped splint covered the freshly set leg. Next, Doc threaded a large curved needle. Several gashes opened disturbingly wide. Finishing the last stitch, Doc wiped his forehead wearily and looked up at Otis. "Why can't you bring me a dog with a sliver in its paw, like everyone else?"

An hour and a half after leaving Bozeman, Brewster and Sean pulled up beside the small cabin. Behind them the busload of searchers and the rescue van pulled in. Brewster crawled out and walked up to the darkened cabin with Sean on his heels. Knocking first from habit, he tried the knob. It turned easily in his hand, and the door swung open. Brewster flicked on the lights.

A rear window was broken. On the table lay a twenty-dollar bill. Bloodstains marked the front room carpet. With a look of concern, Brewster reached down and picked up a bloody shirt. "I hope all this blood is the dog's," he said. "What's happened?"

"I'd be beholden if I knew that myself," Sean

quipped. "This laddy, he's either deserving sainthood or a good thumpin'."

"Let's move," Brewster said, heading for the bus.

Sean followed close on his heels. As men unloaded, several patrol cars pulled up. Brewster walked back and directed one deputy to return to the junction and set up a roadblock to keep out reporters. "When you get set up," he said, "call the captain and let him know what's happening. I don't want anyone past unless they're part of the search. Is that clear?"

"You got it," replied the deputy, crawling back in his car.

Brewster watched the taillights disappear down the canyon. Behind him, Sean was barking orders, and within minutes flashlights poked around outside the cabin looking for sign.

"Over here," cried a voice. "I've got a cycle track headed this way to the road."

With Sean leading the cluster of lights, they spread out and started scouring the road. One searcher stayed with the emergency van for base communications. Every man had a walkie-talkie and wore a small backpack with food and first-aid equipment. An orange reflector patch marked the top of every pack. Nearly half the searchers wore pistols.

The two men with dogs led the group, each flanking a ditch. One small group bunched together and followed the obvious cycle track drifting left and right through the dusty gravel. Others searched along the shoulders and ditches.

The group looked like something out of a space

movie; a monster with thirty beaming legs poking and groping along. As long as they stuck to the road, Brewster was okay. But the road ended after only a mile, and the cycle tracks headed up a trail. The going became steeper and the footing poor. Brewster nursed his bum leg and breathed hard. Ten years ago he could have held his own with any man here. One tiny bullet had changed all that.

After they had climbed three or four miles, Brewster shined his light at his watch—almost three o'clock. The wind had picked up to a stiff, cold breeze. He coaxed his collar up around his ears. It had been two hours since they left the cabin. Had they not been tracking the boy, the moon, now high above the trees, would have made a flashlight unnecessary.

Ahead the group stopped and milled around. Excited whispers filled the air. Brewster, who had been limping and wheezing along behind, pushed to the front. Several voices broke out.

"Where did the tracks go?"

"They left the trail."

"He wouldn't have gone down there."

A thick voice sounded. "Hold it! What's that?"

Lights shined over the bank. Several searchers scurried down the steep edge. Sean followed them but held up his hand to the remaining group. "Stop your bones," he called quietly. "Let's not be wrecking the precious few tracks we have." He motioned Brewster to his side.

Still huffing, Brewster stumbled down the bank.

The wreckage of a red motorcycle was plainly visible, as was a sheared-off six-inch tree halfway down the steep embankment.

Sean whistled softly through his teeth. "Our laddy, now he's trying to fly . . . and look at this." He kneeled down and ran his hand over the damp grass, then brought it into the light of the flashlight. His fingers were crimson red.

"That's fresh!" Brewster exclaimed.

"Likely so," Sean said in a hushed tone. "With this dew, it could be an hour or two old, but not more. If our laddy lives through this, he's truly charmed."

Sean pulled out his walkie-talkie. "Base, can you hear me?"

"Roger," came an instant reply.

"The laddy's had himself a wreck but is still running. As bad as he's bleeding, you better bring a stretcher—I'm thinking we'll be needing one. Bring a med-pak and some blankets too."

"Roger."

Brewster knew Sean was worried—a med-pak contained a variety of medical equipment, including splints, a neck brace, and a blood-pressure cuff.

"I'll send someone down the trail to fetch it from you," Sean continued.

"Ten-four."

"How 'bout a chopper?" a voice in the group suggested.

Sean shook his head. "Not now. We're not at the beach. This is over ten thousand feet, and the wind's a blowin'. I'll not risk a chopper on these slopes at night."

Brewster turned to Sean. "What the devil is keeping that boy going?"

Sean stood slowly, looking up the trail. "Maybe luck. Maybe fear."

CHAPTER 28

AFTER TAKING Josh's boots to the station, Libby returned home. She pulled in the yard and slouched forward against the steering wheel. The only light came from the kitchen window, and she stared at it morosely.

Something was happening. Brewster wouldn't say what, except that they were following up a lead. What kind of lead would have searchers headed out in the middle of the night? And why were they using trail hounds? Brewster would only promise to call her in the morning.

When she left the house earlier, Sam had been asleep. He hadn't even heard Brewster's phone call. Never in her life had Libby felt so alone. She'd lost her husband as surely as she had lost her two sons.

She felt weary. Weary of curiosity seekers and reporters, weary of holding her temper, weary of hurting and caring and being lonely. Lately she even feared entering her own home. Once love and hope warmed those walls; now anger and despair made them stark and cold. She stared numbly into the blackness.

The yellow moon turned cotton white as it crawled upward, disappearing out of sight above the cab. Crickets chorused along the fence. For two hours Libby sat in the darkened drive, afraid to enter the house. Finally, in a daze, she stepped from the pickup and headed for the house. Tonight would end as every other night had since Josh ran away. Sleep would come only when she was so exhausted she could not fight it. Then she would wake early, before sunup, feeling numb.

She ached with sadness and despair. Why wouldn't they tell her if they had sighted Josh? Who could she talk to? In quiet urgency she entered the house and crossed the kitchen. Glancing nervously at the wall clock, she picked up the phone. It was one-thirty in the morning—nobody liked being called at this time of night. But she desperately needed to reach outside of her prison. Maybe she could call Otis. With no notion what to say, she started dialing.

Over and over the phone rang, and she imagined Otis growing more angry. But she felt certain he would be home—he never went anywhere. Libby slouched forward on the table, cradling her cheeks in her hands and sandwiching the phone tightly to her ear. The repeated buzzing mesmerized her and coaxed her back into her daze.

When she started to her senses, she looked up at the clock. She had let the phone ring at least half an hour. Why didn't Otis answer? What was wrong? She bit at her lower lip. The world was closing her out. Frantically, she pulled out the phone number

Brewster had given her. He'd said she could call the captain anytime, day or night. Maybe he had heard something. Shaking with desperation, she dialed.

A man's voice answered. "Hello, Gallatin County Sheriff's Office."

"Hello. This is Libby McGuire. Is this the captain?" she asked.

"No, ma'am. This is Deputy Daniels, duty officer. One moment please, I'll get the captain."

Shortly, a firm, controlled voice came on. "Hello, this is Captain Adams. May I help you?"

"This is Libby McGuire. I . . . ah, wanted to know if you've heard anything about Josh?"

"No, I'm sorry, we haven't yet. We'll call you as soon as we do."

Libby felt her hand start to tremble. The man's voice held such control, such indifference. Didn't he realize her only boy was missing? She couldn't take losing a second child. She fought back her frustration. "Where are you searching for him?" she pleaded. "Did someone report seeing him? Please?"

"I'm sorry, Mrs. McGuire. When we know more, we'll contact you. We're doing everything we can."

Libby's voice shook. "Please tell me what you've found. Josh is my only child now. I know something was going on tonight when I left the station."

Libby heard nervous coughing on the phone. "Mrs. McGuire, take it easy. We're just following up another of the many possible leads. You let us worry about the search. As soon as I hear something, I'll let you know."

Libby slammed down the phone. For nearly a week now she'd controlled her emotions. People coddled her. People told her she was holding up so well. Well, she wasn't! She had swallowed too much: too much anger, too much hurt, too much fear and frustration. And what did she have to show for it?

Libby walked over to a mirror in the hallway. She stared at the flat, colorless plane of her face. She was dead. Her dreams were dead. Never again would she smile, or trust, or love.

Libby spun away from the mirror. No! No! No! It couldn't end like this, she wouldn't let it! Strangely, her frantic thoughts cleared and an eerie calm settled in—not like water coming to rest but rather like iron hardening in a mold. She breathed deeply, forcing the air out again with the same control.

She walked upstairs to the bedroom and snapped on the light. Sam lay motionless, sprawled facedown across the bed. His coarse breathing verged on a snore. Libby began to put on clothes she had not worn since winter: heavy cotton jeans, a flannel shirt, wool socks, a tight knit sweater, a down vest.

Sam groaned and rolled over. "What's going on?" he croaked.

"I'm going to find Josh."

Sam wrinkled his face and squinted to focus on his watch. "You can't do that. It's two-thirty in the morning."

"I can do anything I want, Sam McGuire. I'm done with your anger! I'm done with your self-pity! You'd rather drink than save your family—or what's left of it." Libby's voice grew cold and more deliberate. "Tonight I was afraid to come in the house because you might be drunk. I won't live this way. I'm your wife, Sam. Not some dog! Josh is terrified of you—that's why he ran away. God help you if you ever lay a hand on him again."

Libby slammed the door and stormed down the steps. She heard Sam banging around upstairs. He was probably trying to get dressed with a hangover. She pulled on her hiking boots and headed out the door with a pack in her hand. The small daypack used to belong to Tye. Would she someday be using things that used to belong to Josh? The thought made her lips tremble, and she broke into a run.

When she reached the pickup, she climbed in and cranked mercilessly on the starter. The engine surrendered with a cough and a roar. She ground into first gear and stomped on the gas pedal, spinning out of the drive. Sam ran from the house waving his arms. He was barefoot, his shirt open and pants unzipped. Libby glanced back at him and stepped harder on the accelerator.

By the time she reached the sheriff's station, anger had burned up the last of her fear. She charged into the front office.

"Hello, may I help you?" asked the deputy behind the desk. The weariness of working the graveyard shift diluted his smile.

Libby ignored his polite greeting. "Let me talk to the captain," she demanded.

The man appraised her. "One moment please."

Soon the captain walked into the front office, tucking in his shirttail and running a hand through his tousled hair. He looked tired and irritable. "Mrs. McGuire," he said, "what brings you down here? It's nearly three in the morning."

"Tell me something I don't know," Libby said. She leveled her gaze at the stocky, older man. "I want to know what's going on."

"Mrs. McGuire. Like I told you, as soon as—"

"Damn it! You listen to me. I'm not the press. Josh is my child. I want to know what's going on—now!"

"Mrs. McGuire. Be reasonable—"

"No!—I am being reasonable, and I'll give you a chance to be, too, Captain. You have exactly thirty seconds to tell me what's happening. After that I'm driving down to the motels where the news crews are staying. I'll wake everyone of them and tell them something's up—that you're keeping our family in the dark. See how that sets in your craw, or on 'Good Morning America.' "

"Mrs. McGuire, you don't want to do that."

"Captain Adams, you don't want me to do that," Libby mimicked.

Blue veins rose into view on the captain's flushed neck, and he looked away evasively. With a cold stare, Libby regarded the man. He looked torn with emotions.

Breaking the sudden quiet, a radio crackled in the background. Libby could hear a terse voice. "Dispatch. Get the captain on. There's been an accident."

Libby glanced at the captain with surprise. His eyes

lost all defiance, and he motioned her to a chair while he ran to the radio. Libby ignored his gesture and followed him into the back room.

"Go ahead Bozeman Search," the captain snapped.

"We've found a wrecked cycle with a description matching the boy's. It's at the top of Rock Creek near the meadow. He's not around, but there's fresh blood."

Libby grabbed the captain's sleeve. "Josh! Josh is hurt! I'm going to him," she cried. Libby turned and ran for the door.

"Stand by," the captain barked into his mike. "Mrs. McGuire! Wait!"

Libby looked back briefly. "You're not stopping me."

"I'm not trying to, Mrs. McGuire. I'll drive you down with a patrol car. We'll get there faster."

Libby stared at the captain. "Why should I trust you?"

"I'll think up some reason," he said with a tired smile. "But let me drive you down—I know the way. If your boy is hurt, he'll need you."

Libby stared with uncertainty as the captain grabbed his coat.

"Bozeman Search, we're headed your way," the captain snapped into the mike. "I'm bringing the boy's mother."

"Roger. What's your ETA?"

The captain glanced at his watch. "My estimated time of arrival is about . . . five o'clock."

"Ten-four."

The captain slammed the mike into the cradle and followed Libby out the door. Soon they were speeding into the night. As they drove, the captain told her about Otis Sinclair, about the pen-register, about the roadblock and the hurt dog. "The dog should be out of surgery by now," he said. "Deputy Kelly has been ordered to stay with Otis." The captain also explained the details of the search, and why the secrecy.

Libby pressed a fist to her mouth, no longer feeling defiant. "My poor baby," she whispered. "Please hurry."

Otis smiled wearily, looking at his watch. Nearly two hours had passed since he'd arrived at the animal clinic. He watched Doc Chambers rest the dog on a thick pad in the corner. Otis covered her body with a blanket, except her head.

"Hey, Officer!" Otis called loudly. "How are you doing?"

A muffled grunt and the creak of a chair were the only sounds of reply. Otis had voiced his concern on several occasions—pretty much whenever he thought the officer might be falling asleep. Each time, Doc looked up with a wry smile.

Not until they'd started cleaning up did Doc ask any questions. He turned to Otis. "Is this that boy's dog—the one that ran away to the mountains with a cub? Seems to me they said he had a border collie."

Otis nodded and related the evening's events.

"It would be best if someone stayed with the dog the rest of the night to keep an eye on her," said Doc.

A smile crossed Otis's face. "Are your lobby chairs real hard?" he asked. "Maybe even kind of cold?"

Doc faked seriousness. "Yes, I suppose they are at that."

"Good. I'll stay and call you if the dog has problems."

"You're not going to sleep in the lobby, are you?"

"Oh no," Otis said, smiling again. "If we can leave the dog in this room, I'll grab some blankets and make myself a nice warm bed on the operating table."

CHAPTER 29
CHAPTER

AFTER DISCOVERING the cycle, the searchers swarmed ahead into the night. Traces of blood stained the grass and showed as dark flecks on the ground. The men advanced, their dogs tugging and howling on leashes.

At the meadow they split into three smaller groups—one following the hounds, the other two circling the tree line. Brewster sent a deputy with each group. He stayed with Sean and the dogs. Losing this much blood, the boy could never make it up the peak—they had him trapped in the big alpine basin. A pitch of excitement rose among the men. So often their efforts were futile and thankless; the proverbial searching for a needle in a haystack. But once in a while, they found it!

Beside a narrow trickling stream, matted grass and a large stain of blood showed where the boy had stopped. The bent blades made it look as if he had stretched flat on the ground to drink. What kind of injuries did he have?

Lunging on their leashes, the dogs angled left across the large meadow and up the steep slope. Their pitched baying split the night. The searchers grouped closer and closer, whispering with excitement.

Pounding footsteps caused the searchers to turn. The runner sent by Sean to fetch medical equipment appeared out of the dark, winded and gasping. He wore a large pack and carried an aluminum stretcher.

"I'm thinking we're getting close," Sean said.

"If not, you'll end up using the stretcher to get me down," Brewster said, limping along. "Why did the boy have to climb a mountain? Wouldn't it have been easier on everyone if he'd run away down by the river?"

Sean chuckled. "He probably did it just for you."

When they stopped to rest, Brewster looked back to hide his wheezing. Lights flickered below where searchers circled the meadow. The immediate group of men, maybe a dozen, beamed their lights up across the hillside, probing the rocks and shrubs.

"What's that?" someone exclaimed.

Half a dozen lights scissored up at a black, ominous opening. The men started shouting. Sean whistled sharply, and searchers automatically fell in behind him, lowering their voices.

"Hold the dogs down here," Sean ordered. He motioned to the man with the stretcher and med-pack to follow closely. Quietly they advanced, Sean and Brewster leading the way.

Josh had never known such torture. Nor did his tears help ease the raw pain—it had become a maddening, frightful thing. Waves of hot and cold flooded the sleeping bag. Where thoughts once drifted gently in his head, now they attacked him. Mookee Man grew until he was a giant devil standing over the windswept cavern. His father kept striking out at him from the dark, an evil glint in his eye. "Are you calling me a liar?" Sam growled above the wind. Josh cringed again and again.

Horrible things were happening. But nothing hurt or frightened Josh as much as the fierce loneliness. He sobbed. Everyone in the world was terrible and nasty—everybody was against him. His only comfort was cuddled against his side. Josh rested his hand on Pokey.

A stark moon floated in a black bowl of stars, seeming to drift aimlessly. Wind blustered, and softened, and then whipped again. Josh had never known his senses to jumble so. The pain, the wind, his dry mouth, his anger, the ringing in his ears, the loneliness, it all mixed and slurred together, making him sick.

Suddenly the cub tensed under Josh's sweaty hand, then scrambled to its feet and bolted from the bag. Josh grimaced and tried to call Pokey back, but only a muffled grunt came to his throat. The wind had filled with devilish noises. Josh strained to focus on the darkened shadows of the night. Slowly the strange sounds echoed and floated above his bog of confusion. Dogs howled, and voices shouted.

Panic snapped Josh from his tortured stupor, and he lunged. Straining on one elbow, he wiggled clear of the bag. The cold air chilled his skin, and large beads of sweat stung his eyes.

Pokey cowered behind the boulder and peered cautiously into the dark. When the barking sounded louder in the wind, Pokey stood on his hind legs and braced a paw against the rock. His alert eyes glinted in the moonlight.

Josh tried to stand, but his legs buckled. He gasped. All he could think to do was let Pokey go—at least then the cub could try to run for its life. Catching his breath, Josh crawled through the dirt to Pokey's side. He fumbled weakly with the cub's collar as voices and barking pitched louder. Not being able to use both hands frustrated Josh. Finally, with a painful jerk, he opened the buckle.

Pokey stood still.

"Go!" Josh grunted. He shoved at the cub, chasing it away from the rock. Through the darkness, shafts of light sliced at the night. Frantically Josh crawled for the back of the opening—he had to hide. The vague, clumped shadow of his sleeping bag showed on the ground. He ignored it. With his broken arm dragging, he kept moving.

The only way he could crawl was to push with his good leg and drag with his right elbow. This meant scraping his hurt thigh across the dirt. It felt as if he were swimming on his side in water, with sharks biting and ripping at him from below. But nothing mattered anymore because he had set Pokey free— Pokey had escaped.

At last Josh collapsed into the hollowed nook at the back of the cavern. More beams of light danced in the night. Muffled voices murmured above the wind. Josh rolled onto his back, shooting pain up his leg. He bit at his lip to keep from crying out. Then something touched his face, and he jerked. A fuzzy bundle of hair crowded against his cheek: Josh's heart raced—Pokey! He reached up to shove at the cub, but a sea of black flooded his mind and he felt his hand drop.

The searchers crowded the lip of the cavern. Their lights first focused on a fire pit, smoke drifting in the breeze. Searching wider, they found an empty sleeping bag clumped on the ground, also a big waist-high rock with a rope tied around the bottom. Attached to the end was an unbuckled collar. A closer look showed fresh blood glistening in the dirt.

Bunching close, the group moved forward, probing with their flashlights. From the rear of the hollow, two green eyes stabbed the night. Together the searchers all stepped back. In seconds, every light focused inside the hole. Cowering against an unconscious body was a furry black cub, shaking and glaring.

"It's them!" Sean uttered.

Suddenly the cub crouched, woofing, blowing, and clacking its teeth.

"It looks like he's hurt the boy," someone called.

Sean moved toward the cub. "Let's get the bear away from him," he ordered. "Get me that leash and collar. You lads, take off your coats. Hurry it up, the laddy's hurt." Already he had his coat off and held it by the sleeves, hanging like a shield. Brewster carried the leash and collar, motioning for everyone to spread out. With a wall of jackets, the group approached the back of the opening. Two searchers adamantly refused to go near the bear and hung back, shining their flashlights.

"Easy, there. Easy, there," Sean hummed quietly. In the same soothing voice, he issued orders. "If the rascal runs, we'll not let it past. Throw your jacket over its head . . . and if it's convenient, try avoiding its teeth."

They advanced hesitantly, in a half circle. The cub blew through curled lips, its eyes flickering wildly. As the searchers drew closer, hair stood up on the bear's shoulders, and it swatted the ground, again clacking its teeth. Warily it moved sideways away from the downed boy.

"Okay, now back up," another voice ordered. "I can get a clean shot."

Brewster turned to see a stocky man with his pistol drawn, taking aim. Brewster rushed forward and knocked the pistol sideways. Fire spit from the barrel, and a deafening blast jolted the cavern. The bullet ricocheted off a rock and whined into the dark night.

"You fool!" Brewster roared. "You could have hit the boy, or one of us." He breathed fast, his fists clenched.

The group stood silent. With the pistol carrier nursing his wrist, Sean motioned everyone to advance once again. When they had closed within eight feet, the cub lunged. Sean flung his jacket in the cub's face, then dived on it. He knocked the cub over as several men gangpiled on his back. Jackets flailed, and more men heaped on the pile along with Brewster.

"Grab its legs—it's scratching the bejammers out of me," Sean yelled.

"Ouch! It's chewing on me!" someone else screamed from the bottom.

More grunts and curses mixed with the cub's high-pitched bawling. Slowly the stack of thrashing bodies stilled. The cub squalled bloody murder, held down by every claw and hair.

Brewster slipped the collar on and snugged it tight. "Okay, one of you gents hold this leash when we get off," he ordered, pointing at a large man still standing.

The searchers unpiled guardedly. Free of its attackers, the cub bolted back into the hollow. Before anybody could move, it hugged at the boy's leg, shivering.

"Get it away from the boy," Brewster ordered sharply.

The big man yanked hard, and the cub tumbled backward, clawing and bawling. It twisted wildly in circles, then took off chasing the man with the leash. Amidst laughter from the group, the cub stopped at the edge of the cavern. There it sulked, trembling.

"I'd say the two are friends," Sean said, rushing to the boy's side. Brewster followed behind.

Josh groaned.

"Laddy, can you hear me?" Sean asked loudly, kneeling over Josh.

Josh continued to groan and moved his lips as if trying to speak. His left arm was bent grotesquely. A large knob showed under the skin, and blood stained the full length of his right pant leg. His face and arm were scraped and bleeding.

"Cripe. He looks like he's been to hell and back," Brewster said, watching Sean feel for the boy's pulse.

Sean turned his head slightly. "I'm not sure he's made it back yet."

CHAPTER 30

CHAPTER

STANDING IN a circle around the boy, the searchers shined their flashlights. Strain and fatigue showed on their weary faces.

"Jim!" Sean called. "I need you."

A lanky man kneeled quickly by Sean's side as Brewster pulled out his walkie-talkie. "Alpha group, Delta group, we've found him," he announced. "Rendezvous back at the trailhead. We'll bring him down."

He waited for confirmation from the other two search parties, then turned to Sean. "You want a chopper?"

Sean nodded. "If we can get him down to the trailhead, I'm thinking a chopper might land near the gravel road. By then it will be daybreak."

Sean lifted Josh's eyelids and shined a flashlight in his pupils. Josh made a feeble attempt to raise his head. "Easy, laddy. We're here to help you," Sean said softly as he pumped up a blood pressure cuff on Josh's good arm.

As Sean worked over Josh, Brewster keyed his walkie-talkie. "Base, do you read me?"

"Roger, go ahead."

"We're bringing the boy down. Get a chopper in as close to the trailhead as you can."

Sean reached up and grabbed the walkie-talkie from Brewster. "Base, the laddy has possible internal injuries, and he's lost a lot of blood. Give these vitals to the whirly-boys. I'll let you know if anything changes."

"Roger, standing by," came the reply.

"Pulse is one-o-eight," he announced. "Respiration is twenty-four and shallow. Blood pressure, ninety over forty-six." Sean handed the walkie-talkie back and started splinting Josh's arm.

"Okay, Base," Brewster said, "we'll be at the trailhead in about an hour and a half."

Sean spoke sharply. "One hour!"

"Ah, Base, make that one hour," Brewster corrected.

Sean looked up with a thin smile. "The picnic's over—no coffee breaks now."

Strapped to the stretcher and covered with blankets, Josh moaned and moved his lips. Suddenly his eyes came open wide. "Otis, you dirty fink," he grunted. Then his eyes closed again.

"What was that all about?" Sean asked.

"You got me," Brewster said. "How is he?"

"Not good," Sean replied as he stood stiffly. "Not good at all. Okay, men, let's get him down."

In the gray morning air, Brewster stood with Sean, watching the searchers carry the stretcher and Josh's belongings over the rim. A lonesome bawl echoed from behind. Brewster turned and found the cub hunkered at the end of his rope. The large man assigned bear duty stood clinging to the leash, his body tense.

Brewster smiled and walked over. "Would you mind if I led the cub down?"

The man smiled as if he'd been granted reprieve from execution. "Ah, oh, not at all, sir, not at all!" He nearly threw the leash at Brewster, then took off running after the others.

The cub crouched when Brewster pulled. It curled its thin lips and blew forcefully.

"He's not blowing out birthday candles," Sean quipped. "With your bad leg, are you up to this?"

Brewster nodded. "This way I have an excuse for goin' slow."

Sean smiled wearily. "Ahh, a true saint. See you at the bottom then."

"You got it," Brewster said, yawning. As Sean trotted off down the hill, Brewster checked his watch—a little after five. Without notice the pale lush glow of morning had settled softly like a halo among the peaks. As he watched the searchers and stretcher cross the meadow, Brewster considered his situation: standing here at eleven thousand feet on a mountain, four miles from any road, five o'clock in the morning, and holding a small bear on a leash. "How did I ever get into this?" he grumbled, tugging on the rope.

The cub glared intently, stumbling in tow on stiff legs.

Libby and the captain sped into the night, winding south along the gorge into Paradise Valley. Libby sat rigid, watching the mile markers flash past. So lost was she in her thoughts, she no longer noticed the gray metal sky, or the crackling radio, or the captain's soft, weary smile.

Dawn streaked the horizon as they reached the Tom Miner pulloff. Swerving and bouncing, the patrol car pulled onto the gravel road.

"Right ahead we'll be coming to the roadblock," said the captain. Even as he spoke, nearly a dozen cars and vans came into sight at the Rock Creek junction. "What's this, a convention?" he muttered.

A deputy ran up to their window as they pulled up. "Am I glad to see you, Captain," he exclaimed. "About an hour after I got here, these reporters started showing up. You'd have thought we advertised this thing in the paper."

The captain shook his head. "Just keep them out of our hair."

The deputy smiled and did a stiff-legged salute. "Yes, sir, Cap'n." Then he motioned them past.

Several reporters scrambled from their vehicles and came running. They waved their arms and yelled questions. The captain quickly rolled up his window and sped off. Libby heard the shouting fade away as they bounced wildly up the rutted, narrow road. Soon the captain picked up his mike. "Base, do you read?"

"This is Base—go ahead."

"This is Captain Adams. I just passed the road-block. Any news on the boy yet?"

"Yes, sir. They've found him."

Libby gasped and held her breath.

"How is he?" asked the captain.

"Alive, but I guess he's pretty rough. They're on their way down with him now. A helicopter's due here—ETA, fifteen minutes."

"Okay, we'll be there soon."

"Ten-four."

The captain wiped his brow with his sleeve and looked over at Libby. "How you doing?" he asked.

Libby bit at her lower lip and tried to hold back the tears.

"Here," he said, handing her a handkerchief.

Libby smothered her face in the small cloth and wept. Not until they pulled to a stop did she look up, sniffling.

"He's in good hands," assured the captain.

Libby nodded and stepped wearily from the patrol car. The fresh morning air felt good. She drew a deep breath and looked up toward the woods. In the distance a dull thumping sound touched the air.

A man poked his head out the back of a big white Search and Rescue van. "The chopper's coming!" he shouted.

The captain nodded and waved acknowledgment.

Libby stared up at the vacant sky. They were standing in a clearing by the trailhead. Except for the helicopter's drumbeat echoing over the treetops, the cold air was quiet. Libby toyed nervously with a strand of her hair. "Please call and ask how Josh is," she said, turning to the captain.

The captain nodded. He adjusted his walkie-talkie. "Mountain Search, can you read me?"

Sean's huffing voice came back with a crackle. "I read you, Captain."

"How is the boy?"

"The laddy's not feeling too perky."

"What's your ETA?" asked the captain.

"About fifteen minutes if I can keep these lads from loafing. Now, Brewster, he might be a week or two."

"Why is that?"

"He's bringing down the cub . . . voluntarily, I must add," Sean laughed. "Ah, yes, I can see it now—Bingham's Bear Delivery Service. Has a nice ring don't you think, Captain?"

Libby smiled in spite of herself. From the sound of the man's voice, she could tell they were moving fast and hard. The dull thrumming of the helicopter grew louder. She looked back at the sky. Above the timbered hill a red pod appeared, swooping toward them like a huge bumblebee. The thumping became a steady, thunderous clap, and Libby felt the captain grab her arm to pull her back from the clearing.

Wind swept the grass flat in a big circle as the helicopter settled roughly to the ground with a high-pitched whine. Someone with a helmet and visor jumped from the red chopper and ran toward them, head ducked low. The runner wore a blue jumpsuit and carried a large flight bag. The deafening whine softened as the helicopter's big blades whipped slower.

The blue-clad crew member turned out to be a woman. "I'm Kathy Barret, RN," she shouted, pulling off her helmet. "Is the boy down yet?"

The captain shook his head and looked at his watch. "His ETA is ten minutes."

"Okay," shouted the wiry nurse, "I've got things to get ready." She flashed ten fingers at the pilot as she ran back toward the helicopter.

Time seemed to stop. Libby kept looking at her watch and then at the trailhead. This couldn't be happening—all these people, the van, the roadblock, the media, the police cars, the helicopter—all for her little Josh? She knew he had spunk, but what in the world had he done to get into this kind of trouble? Maybe none of this would have happened if she had been a better mother. Libby found herself shifting back and forth on her feet and wringing her hands.

"I see 'em coming!" shouted the captain.

Libby looked up at the trailhead and saw a group of men spilling from the trees. In the center, four of them carried a stretcher at a trot. Soon other men fanned out into the clearing, running and shouting.

Libby ran to meet them. "Josh!" she screamed, crowding in beside the moving stretcher. She barely recognized him. His face was scraped and swollen and covered with dirt. And his eyes were closed.

The captain caught up to her and pulled her away. "We have to keep out of their way," he said. She grabbed desperately for the stretcher, but he held her. "Please," he said.

"That's my baby. That's my baby," she cried, twisting out of his grip. She ran to where the group was loading Josh on the helicopter. "I'm going with him," she screamed.

The captain ran up to the flight nurse. "This is the boy's mother," he shouted.

"Okay," said the nurse. "Go around the other side. The pilot will load her."

The helmeted pilot helped Libby up onto a canvas bench seat facing the rear. He handed her a set of headphones and tightened her seat belt roughly.

Shortly the nurse scrambled aboard and gave the pilot a thumbs-up. "Let's go! Let's go!" she hollered.

The engine revved back into a piercing whine and the big chopper lifted off. Libby looked fearfully around the small cabin. As the ground dropped away, she watched the nurse work over Josh. His eyes opened briefly, then closed. A couple of times he moved his arm weakly. The second time, Libby reached over and held his hand. The nurse looked up and smiled, but Libby saw worry in her eyes.

CHAPTER 31

CHAPTER

LIBBY CLUNG to Josh's hand as the nurse kept working over him. The helicopter vibrated with a deafening *thup thup thup* as hills and meadows drifted past. More and more often, Josh opened his eyes. Finally he tilted his head and gave Libby a blank stare. She squeezed his hand harder. Josh moved his lips, but the shrill whining of the engine drowned his voice.

Libby felt helpless, as if her life had been shattered. She was fighting and clawing to save the bits and pieces. Tye's death had been one big piece she could never replace. What other pieces would be missing before this was all over?

When it seemed they would never reach the hospital, the helicopter banked steeply and started descending. A landing pad floated into view, surrounded by a group of people. As the copter settled to the ground with a rough jar, several people in white coats rushed out, their heads ducked low.

"You can stay with him!" the flight nurse shouted to Libby. "But give us room until we get him inside."

Libby nodded reluctantly, letting go of Josh's hand.

She unbuckled herself and crawled stiffly from the helicopter. Deliberately she followed behind the stretcher. So absorbed was she with Josh, she did not see the horde of reporters and camera people until they folded around the stretcher at the edge of the pad.

"Let us through! Get out of the way!" the nurse shouted. As they rushed Josh across the lawn and into the emergency room, the group turned on Libby and blocked her path.

"Mrs. McGuire. How is Josh doing?"

"Can you tell us where they found him?"

"Where is the cub?"

"Did they kill it?"

Libby looked into the swarm of faces, microphones, and clicking cameras. She panicked and covered her ears. "Leave me alone!" she screamed, lowering her head and bulling through the crowd. She bumped aside microphones and ran after Josh.

Concern pried at Libby's thoughts as she watched the medical people working. They had Josh's clothes removed and had begun cleaning and examining him. Libby could see his broken arm and the gaping gash in his thigh. A large bruise stained his chest. Smaller scrapes and cuts spattered his body, and his face puffed with redness. But worse, he looked gaunt and haggard.

She approached Josh, but the nurse stopped her. "Excuse us," said the nurse, "we need to take him for X rays."

Libby trembled as they wheeled Josh on a gurney

into a side room. Where was Sam? She looked at her watch—seven o'clock. He was probably in bed sleeping off his hangover. From the X-ray room Libby heard Josh screaming, "They shot Pokey! They shot Pokey!" Quieter voices tried to pacify him. Libby paced the floor. Could it be possible? Why would they have shot the cub? Again Josh screamed, "Otis, you fink! You rat fink!" Libby trembled. What was going on in her son's mind? Otis had been his best friend.

Soon they returned Josh to the emergency room and started mending his leg. A doctor clipped the developed X rays to a lighted glass and examined them. Shaking his head, he turned to Josh. "You're a lucky boy," he said.

"Why?" Josh asked with a pout.

"Your arm's broken, but your ribs are only bruised."

"I don't care about my ribs, or arm, or nothin'. They killed Pokey."

"Josh," Libby cried, "all we care about is you."

Josh grew quiet. "Nobody cared about Pokey," he mumbled.

Libby caught the doctor's arm as he passed. "Will he be all right?" she asked.

The doctor nodded. "We think so. You have quite a trouper, Mrs. McGuire."

The nurse took Libby's arm. "We'd like you to wait in the next room while we work on his arm," she said.

"Will you anesthetize him?" Libby asked fearfully.

"We'll give him a local in the arm, but he'll stay awake," said the nurse.

Libby set her chin. "Then I want to stay with him. That's where his mother should be."

With a nod from the doctor, the nurse reluctantly agreed.

Libby stroked Josh's sweaty forehead as they set his arm. Each time he screamed or screwed his eyes shut with pain, Libby bit at her lip.

"How does it feel now, young man?" asked the doctor when he had finished wrenching on the arm.

Josh's voice sounded resentful. "Why did they have to kill Pokey?" he said. "He didn't do anything."

Brewster was still hobbling down the trail with the cub in tow when he heard the helicopter leave. A hundred times he'd regretted offering to take the cub—about as many times as he'd been charged and nipped. He'd decided there was no such thing as a small biting bear.

When the cub finally quit attacking, it took a notion to playing. This was almost as bad. It swatted at Brewster's heels, sending him stumbling. Then it jumped and nipped at his rump. A dozen healthy bites had Brewster walking backward to guard his backside. The cub circled playfully, watching for any opportunity.

However irksome the cub was, Brewster felt sorry for it. The little fellow's antics were almost childlike. Its bawl sounded like a mournful plea. Brewster could only imagine what the cub had been through in the last week. And all for naught if what they said about its disposal was true.

The walkie-talkie crackled, "Brewster, might you make it down in this lifetime?"

Brewster stopped and stretched out his antenna. "Blazes, Sean!" he answered. "This confounded animal's going to chew me into hamburger first."

"Where are you?"

Brewster looked around. "Beats me, I'm passing an old forest fire burn area on my left."

"Ah, you're nearly here. The cub must be pulling you."

"Sean, what's happening down there?"

"The mum, she came up with the captain and flew out with her laddy. Everyone's gone now. I'm lying here restin' and waiting for you."

"Ten-four."

Minutes later Brewster and the cub stumbled out onto the road and found Sean resting against a tree.

Sean looked up with a yawn. "I was feeling sorry for the little one, having to pull you down the mountain."

Brewster mopped his forehead with a sleeve and led the cub over beside the patrol car. "I can't remember when I've been so blame hungry, tired, and thirsty in my life," he said, tying the rope to a door handle.

Sean crawled to his feet. "There's a cooler in there with some food."

Brewster nodded appreciatively. After retrieving it,

he set it on the ground, eagerly removing the cover. The sulking cub perked its ears. It sniffed the air and advanced boldly. Before Brewster could move, the cub pounced on the cooler, scattering sandwiches, cookies, and chips.

"Hey, get away from that!" Brewster shouted, giving the cub a shove.

It spun, lightning fast, nipping Brewster's wrist. Then it hunched back over the food, gulping at it and growling.

"I'm starting to feel like a chew toy," Brewster said, nursing his wrist. "Would you pull him away? I'm tired of getting bit."

"Oh, no! I'm not hungry," Sean said, faking seriousness. "Better let him eat, or he'll keep this up." Nonchalantly, Sean opened the trunk and took out a tire iron. "This might help," he said, walking around toward the cub.

"Oh, Sean. Don't do that," Brewster said quickly.

Sean ignored him and continued to the front of the patrol car, where he bent over and pried off a hubcap. He emptied a canteen into the shiny bowl and set it next to the cub. "Shouldn't I give him water?" Sean asked with a wink.

Brewster sighed as the cub dived for the hubcap, slurping and sucking until the water was gone. Then it hunched back over the few remaining cookies, still growling.

"Would you mind putting him in the car?" Brewster asked, when the cub had finished.

"I'd not think of it," Sean said. "You're his friend."

Brewster scowled, rubbing his wrist. "Friend, my foot."

"Here, try this," Sean said, reaching in his jacket pocket. He tossed over the crumpled remains of a candy bar.

Brewster untied the cub and gave it a whiff of the chocolate. Then, before he could get bit again, he tossed the wrapper into the backseat of the patrol car. The cub scrambled in, and Brewster slammed the door.

A heavy metal grating barricaded the rear seat from the front. Brewster shook his head. "That grate's protected me from many a drunk," he said. "I never thought I'd see the day it would protect me from a bear."

Brewster squirmed uncomfortably as he drove, rubbing gingerly at his sore posterior. He'd heard of duty before honor, but this was ridiculous. He noticed the sun poking above the trees and looked at his watch—seven o'clock. It would be eight-thirty by the time they got back to Bozeman.

Thoughts of the cub troubled Brewster. The boy had risked his life to save it. And he'd failed.

"What's planned for the cub when we get back?" Sean asked.

Brewster drove some distance before answering. "I don't know," he said sadly. "It's going to be hard turning it over to Deke Mizner. Maybe Otis Sinclair has an idea—if he's still talking to me."

CHAPTER 32

CHAPTER

OTIS AWOKE, confused by the strange surroundings of the animal clinic. When his thoughts cleared, he smiled. Sleep on the operating table had been quite comfortable—better than a hard chair. He crawled down and knelt beside Mud Flap. The small dog breathed regularly, eyes opened wide. But her tail remained still. The spirit seemed drained from her scrawny body. In a way, Otis felt like the dog—alive, but so what!

Otis heard a car pulling in the front lot—probably Doc Chambers. He also heard a groan and a rough cough from the waiting room. A chair creaked and Deputy Kelly appeared in the doorway. His uniform was crumpled and his hair on end.

"Good morning, Rambo," Otis said cheerfully to the bedraggled deputy.

The officer scowled without answering and walked over to the desk. Picking up the phone, he dialed. "Dispatch," he said, "let me talk to the captain . . ." The deputy worked his fingers through his knotted hair as he waited. "Morning, Captain . . . huh, they what? . . . They found the boy? Well what am I supposed to do with Sinclair?" Deputy Kelly's voice turned into a whine. "Release him—you mean I just slept in a chair all night so I could let him go? . . . Ah, no sir, I didn't know you'd been up all night. Okay, sir. Yes, sir."

Deputy Kelly slammed down the phone as Doc Chambers entered the room. The officer glowered at Otis. "Mr. Sinclair, you're free to go," he snapped.

Otis gave Doc a wink and smiled at the officer. "Excuse my saying so, but it appears you're the one free to leave."

The deputy stomped out, rattling the windows when he slammed the door.

"How's she doing?" Doc asked, kneeling to look at the dog.

Otis shook his head. "She doesn't seem too excited about living."

"We'll take some X rays this morning," Doc said. "But I suggest you keep her at your house. She needs TLC more than medical treatment."

Otis agreed. After leaving the animal clinic, he returned home and made a bed for Mud Flap on the living room floor. The small dog sported a cast and several large bandages. She seemed to rest comfortably, but her eyes stared vacantly into space, despondent. Otis stroked her forehead. All he could do now was wait. As he stood, the phone rang. Thinking the call might be from Libby, Otis answered sooner than he preferred, and more gently. "Hello," he said.

"Hello, this is Brewster. I need to talk to you."

Otis regretted having softened his characteristic

growl. Immediately he mustered the gravel back into his voice. "Bingham, why can't you leave me alone?"

"Just listen to me a minute. We found Josh—"

"What a surprise—you followed me right to him."

"Otis, I have the cub, and I need your help."

"Gimme a break! You just want me to do your dirty work for you. Call the Fish and Game yourself."

"Isn't there something else we can do? You know what Deke Mizner will do with the cub."

Otis left his growl intact. "I have no authority over the cub."

"I know that. But Josh nearly killed himself trying to save the little rascal. I figured—"

"What? Is Josh hurt?"

"Yes. He was in pretty rough shape when they flew him out. He wrecked his motorcycle."

Otis swallowed, his thoughts confused. This wasn't supposed to have happened. Josh was just being a silly kid, and for a while it had been fun watching the bureaucrats sweat. But it had been a game— nothing to die for.

"Otis, if I turn that cub over, everything the boy did is wasted. He's got the media all stirred up. Shoot, even the governor called. Please, can you think of anything to do?"

"That's all I've ever done my whole life, try and figure out what to do," Otis said. When Brewster failed to answer, Otis gave in. "Ah, go ahead, bring him over. I don't know what I can do, though."

"Thanks," Brewster said, his voice subdued. "I'm calling from the Paradise Valley. I'll be there within the hour. And Otis . . . I need to tell you one more thing."

"What's that?"

"The boy seemed upset with you."

Otis frowned. "What do you mean upset? Was he talking?"

"Not really. He just mumbled a few words."

"Well, what did he say?"

Brewster hesitated. "His words were . . . 'Otis, you dirty fink.' "

Otis gripped the phone and bunched his lips. "Probably figures I turned him in."

"I'll explain to him what happened," Brewster said.

"Yeah, you'll make things all better, won't you. That's why you called me to take the cub." Otis slammed down the phone. With a heavy sigh he walked over to his desk and pulled out a dusty card file.

One by one he leafed through the yellowed cards, pausing first at one, then another. For years, while he taught at the university, this had been his life: a game of lobbying names and positions. Otis stopped and stared at one frayed and worn card in particular. There were two numbers listed: one labeled Switchboard, one labeled Direct. A large red star marked the upper left corner. Otis looked hard at the card. He'd sworn never to use this one again.

Hesitantly he reached and picked up the phone. His hand trembled and for a moment he almost hung up. Then, stiffly, he dialed the number listed under

Direct. This man had fought him nose to nose on dozens of environmental issues in the state legislature—and look at what had become of them both. Otis let go of the last digit and his eyes settled on the typed name at the top of the card: Governor Cecil Harden.

Despite the early hour, a dulcet voice answered. "Hello, governor's office."

"This is Otis Sinclair. I want to talk to Cecil."

"Is the governor expecting your call?"

"I don't have much stomach for appointments anymore, young lady. I'm calling regarding the McGuire boy and the cub, and to save Cecil one whale of a lot of trouble."

"Let me check if he's in yet, Mr. Sinclair."

"You're his secretary," Otis spit. "You know jolly well if he's in or not. Play whatever game you want, but in thirty seconds I'm hanging up."

"One moment, Mr. Sinclair," the lady stammered.

Otis burned with resentment. He was tasting again the very poison that had wasted thirty years of his life. Man created government and built big buildings and arbitrated until he thought of himself as God. Was it a committee's decision how much pollution a million dollars was worth? Were animals something to be budgeted like tax dollars?

A voice interrupted Otis's bitter reflection. "Hello, this is Governor Harden."

Otis drew a deep breath. "Cecil, this is Otis Sinclair."

"Otis Sinclair! Now there's a name I haven't heard

in years. If you'll excuse me, Otis, I'm busy at the moment."

"Too busy to be reelected?" Otis said.

There was a nervous cough. "What is it I can do for you?" asked the cautious voice.

Otis nearly laughed. Politicians always asked what they could do for you. What it really boiled down to was what served their interests—only then did they lift a finger. He steadied his voice. "Listen. You and I butted heads for years, until I got a sore skull. I'm not calling to lock horns again. I'm calling to save your tail."

"I wasn't aware my tail needed saving," the governor said, his voice becoming guarded.

"The McGuire boy has been found, and the cub is going to be confiscated. I believe you're aware of that," Otis said.

"Yes, I was notified nearly an hour ago. What does this have to do with you?"

"Never mind me. District Fish and Game Administrator Deke Mizner has jurisdiction over the cub's disposal. With him the cub won't stand a chance— the man's a ladder climber." Otis let the term *ladder climber* come off his tongue thick with contempt, just in case the shoe fit more than one foot.

"Can't he send the cub to a zoo or something? Why are you calling me?" asked the governor.

Otis coughed. "Deke couldn't care less about saving the cub. Not a zoo in the country wants a small, scrappy western black bear. They all look for the big, impressive eastern bruins. Because the cub isn't wounded, Deke will send it to the state laboratories for disease studies—in effect, for destruction. The media will burn you at the stake if I let them know you allowed that to happen."

"It's not my decision," the governor said.

"You're in charge of all state affairs. If you'll pardon my saying so, Cecil, a governor's recommendation can change tomorrow's weather."

The governor chuckled. "What are you suggesting I do?"

Otis wiped perspiration from his forehead. "I was hoping you'd ask me that."

Brewster sighed with relief after talking to Otis. He'd called from a roadside phone to give Otis time to prepare a cage. That is, if Otis agreed to take the cub—which he had. But now what? The cub's frightened eyes haunted Brewster.

An hour later he swung through Bozeman and headed out toward Otis's cabin. Sean rode along, staring tiredly out the dusty window. Suddenly a sour look appeared on his face. "Ahh, man. Are you smelling what I am?"

Brewster sniffed and wrinkled his nose. He looked back in time to see the cub scramble across the rear seat to avoid its own mess. "Aw, gimme a break," Brewster bellowed. "Couldn't you hold it just one more mile?"

The cub cowered, and Sean looked over reprovingly. "Shame—now you scared the little fellow."

"I don't believe this is happening," Brewster

moaned. "I spend half the morning towing him off a mountain, he chews on me like bubble gum, and then eats my breakfast. I'll probably get a reprimand for taking him out to Sinclair's, and now this."

Sean slapped Brewster's shoulder. "You're the lucky one, huh."

Not wanting to do battle with the scrappy cub again, Brewster drove the last half mile to the cabin with windows wide open—it didn't help. After pulling into the yard, his disposition took another blow.

Otis saw Pokey's accomplishments and let go with a short bark of a laugh. "So that's why you wanted to bring him out here," he snorted.

Brewster tried to hold his temper. "Have any idea how we can save the cub?" he asked.

"We?" Otis exclaimed sarcastically. Then he turned serious. "You let me worry about the cub. It looks like you'll be spending the next week in a car wash."

"Real funny," Brewster muttered.

Otis approached the sullen cub, cooing, his body crouched eye level with the small animal.

"Be careful," Brewster said, rubbing at his tender wrist.

Gently Otis reached his hand forward and let the cub smell his fingers. Brewster and Sean watched in amazement. While the cub sniffed, Otis scratched under its chin, then its neck. In minutes the cub crawled forward. Otis calmly lifted the heavy black bundle and carried it over to a chest-high chain-link enclosure. Softly he spoke to it.

"The only reason that happened," Brewster grumbled to Sean, "is because the cub was tuckered out from biting me."

They followed Otis to the pen—already food and water were set out in dishes. But the cub sulked to the farthest corner.

"He's got the same blues as the dog," Otis said, returning with them to the patrol car.

"How is the dog?" Brewster asked.

"Physically, okay . . . mentally, not worth a hoot. How is Josh?"

Brewster shook his head. "We don't know yet. I plan on heading over there after I finish my report at the station. The captain scheduled a noon news conference at the hospital. After that I'm going home to bed."

Before leaving the yard, Brewster spent several minutes wiping off the car seat.

"Ah, could I offer to buy you breakfast?" Sean asked.

Brewster felt green and gave Sean a vile look.

Sean ignored the look and broke into a belly laugh, slapping his leg.

CHAPTER
CHAPTER 33

OTIS WATCHED Brewster leave the drive, then returned to the house to finish breakfast. Out of habit, he turned on the television for the morning news and ate his food with the TV droning in the background. He paid little attention until he heard something about a cub. Quickly he turned up the volume.

Repeating our lead story this hour. Earlier this morning searchers in Montana found Josh McGuire, the young boy who ran away with a bear cub to save its life. It is believed the boy has been involved in some form of accident. The extent and cause of his injuries are not known at this time. This video footage was taken a short while ago in Bozeman.

Otis watched the screen intently. Amid screaming reporters and camera people, a fuzzy picture showed a stretcher being rushed from a helicopter into a hospital.

The story continued:

The cub was reportedly taken to Bozeman. We've contacted Fish and Game officials, who deny any knowledge

of the cub's whereabouts. A news conference is scheduled at Bozeman Deaconess Hospital at twelve noon.
We will carry that live. And now for a message from our
sponsor.

Otis turned the volume down and started making
breakfast. How had this whole thing blown up like
this? A few days ago it had started with a scared voice
asking what to feed a cub.

As Otis finished eating, he heard a vehicle pull in
his drive. Who was it now? This place had gotten
more popular than a dance floor on prom night. Otis
wiped a napkin across his mouth and pushed out
from the table. Before he could make it to the door,
the visitor knocked viciously, continuing to hammer
away even as Otis called, "I'm coming!"

"Hey! Hey! Hey!" Otis shouted, opening the door.
"If you want to knock the place down, I'll get you a
crowbar."

Deke Mizner stood there angrily, without apology.
"Do you have the cub?" he demanded.

"Why would I have it?" Otis said innocently.

"Because nobody else seems to. Now, do you have
the cub?" Deke roared.

Otis nodded, looking down at Deke's pistol belt.
"The cub is here, but I suggest you leave it alone."

"This is my jurisdiction. I'm having your Fish and
Game license revoked for this," Deke said, heading
for the pens.

Otis spoke calmly. "I still wouldn't mess with the
cub if I were you."

Those words seemed to set Deke off. He was not used to having his authority questioned. He spun on Otis. "If you're refusing to surrender an animal to authorities, I'll have you arrested."

Otis remained calm. "I wouldn't think of withholding game from the proper authority," he said, looking at his watch. "He should be here soon."

Deke paused, a question in his eyes. Then anger flooded his glare, and he turned and headed for the pens. "I am the proper authority," he spit over his shoulder. "And I'm here to get the cub. Don't try to stop me."

"You're making a mistake, Deke," Otis said, his voice calm but terse.

Deke didn't look back again. He walked down the line of cages until he spotted the cub huddled against the wire, shaking and looking pitiful. Deke grabbed the rope from where it hung on a nail. "You're a fool, Otis," he shouted back, "to lose your license over one pathetic animal."

Deke stooped and opened the door, holding the rope in one hand. As he entered, the cub hunkered against the pen wall, blowing and woofing. Deke looked back. Otis watched intently from near the cabin. This seemed to anger Deke even more. He crawled closer.

Otis heard a car pull in the yard. He nodded to the man who crawled out. "Morning, Cecil—or do you like being called Governor? How was your flight from Helena?"

"Good enough—but not what I had planned for this morning. You owe me one for this."

"Saving your neck from the media doesn't make me beholden in my book," Otis shot back.

The governor ignored the comment. "What's going on here?" he asked, pointing to the green Fish and Game blazer.

"That's Deke Mizner," Otis said, gesturing to where Deke had crawled in the cub's cage. "He's come to take the cub."

"Leave the cub alone!" the governor called to Deke.

Deke looked back and squinted into the morning sun. "Stay out of this whoever you are," he shouted.

Otis followed the governor over to the row of cages. As they approached, Deke reached for the cub. Like lightning, the cub lunged and bit his hand, twisting and clawing.

Deke let go and moved backward, his fingers bleeding. He backed right into the door's low cross brace and smacked his head. "You good-for-nothin' crow bait," he muttered, pulling out his pistol.

"Put it down, Deke! . . . I said put it down!" the governor snapped.

Deke hesitated, looking back. Slowly recognition came to his eyes, but he did not lower the gun. "Ah, Governor, what are you doing here?" he stammered.

"Put it down!" growled the governor.

Deke lowered the pistol hesitantly, his hand shaking. "But, Governor, this is my jurisdiction. They brought the cub out here instead of surrendering it to headquarters. Now I've tracked it down."

The governor spoke in a cold tone. "I talked with the state director this morning. He said you were made aware of the public relations nightmare this cub has become. But you still don't seem to understand. You kill that cub now and Otis is right, the press would string us all up. I'm sorry, but I won't pay for your stupidity."

"But, Governor, if we give in on this one—"

Otis interrupted. "You really don't get it, do you, Deke?" His voice pitched with bitterness. "That cub is more than twenty-five pounds of meat and hair. He's a shred of our dignity. He's the hope we have for survival—the reason you wear that uniform. The boy and this cub have done more for this planet in a week than you have in a career. They've given people all across the United States hope for a better world."

"Oh, get off your high horse, Sinclair," Deke spit. "You think this is Disneyland? You don't really—"

The governor took a step forward. "Bite it, Deke," he said. "You're through with the Montana State Fish and Game Department. Your authority is over . . . now leave!"

CHAPTER 34

CHAPTER

LIBBY WATCHED as the last length of plastered tape was applied to Josh's cast.

"Libby!" a voice called.

She turned to find Brewster Bingham in the opened door of the emergency room. He looked haggard in a dirt-smudged uniform.

She walked over. "Brewster! What are you doing here?"

"I came for the news conference and to see how Josh is doing. Is he okay?"

Libby hesitated. How could she describe Josh's indifference and the emptiness she felt? Finally she nodded. "Yeah, I guess so."

"Is something wrong?"

"No, he's fine." She turned her head away.

"What's wrong, Libby? Is it Sam?"

"Sam—no, I don't even know where he is," she said, hanging her head. Then she spoke quietly. "It's Josh. He acts like I'm a stranger."

Brewster smiled softly. "He's been through an awful lot. Give him some time."

At that moment the doctor walked past, and

Brewster stopped him. "Excuse me, Doctor. I'm Deputy Bingham. We've scheduled a news conference for noon. Can you give the press a statement on Josh's medical condition?"

The man nodded.

"One more thing. Can I talk to Josh a minute?"

"You can try," the doctor said, looking at Libby. "Would that be okay, Mrs. McGuire?"

Libby nodded.

They walked together over to where Josh sat in a wheelchair. He wore a blue gown and sat with his head bowed. His hair was still tangled and matted.

"So you're Josh McGuire," Brewster said, smiling broadly.

Josh showed no response.

"I'm Brewster Bingham, head of the Bozeman Search and Rescue. I have some things I need to tell you."

Josh lifted his head, his eyes blinking back tears. "Why did you shoot Pokey? He didn't do nothin'."

"What? What are you talking about?"

"I heard you shoot him," Josh blurted.

Libby remembered talk of the cub at the trailhead. But she also saw the look in Josh's eyes. He was telling the truth—that much she knew. She touched Brewster's arm. "Why did you shoot the cub?"

Brewster seemed surprised by her words. "Oh . . . no! One of the searchers tried to, but I knocked his shot wide." He smiled lightly. "In fact, I've got the sorest bottom in the room to remind me how alive it is."

Josh looked directly at her. "Mom, they killed Pokey!" he cried. "They killed him."

Libby felt confused, and her mind raced. The sheriff's department had lied to her before, and they had surely withheld information. Were they covering up now?

Brewster paused. "Pokey and Mud Flap are both fine. They're with Otis, and he—"

"Otis is a fink!" Josh pouted.

"Why do you say that?" Brewster asked.

"He told me he was alone and wouldn't tell anyone. The dirty fink!"

"Otis didn't turn you in, Josh," Brewster said.

"Yes he did!" Josh said, raising his voice. "He said he came to the cabin alone. And then I saw two cars leave the canyon."

"That's all my fault, not Otis's. Last night I had a deputy follow him. Otis didn't know anything about it until he left the cabin. Then I had him stopped."

"Arrested?" Libby asked.

"Well, not exactly. Forcibly escorted."

Josh remained silent.

"Finding you has been my job," Brewster said. "During the search, Otis had me so mad I could strangle him. Do what you want, Josh, but don't blame him. Otis is trying to help you save Pokey. And now, so am I."

Josh looked up, distrust shrouding his face. He jutted his lower lip out, then turned away.

Libby looked at Brewster, searching for some sign of a crack in his integrity. She found none. And yet,

Josh was not one to lie. She knew him better than this deputy.

She knelt and held Josh's hand. "I believe you, Josh," she said. Then she looked at Brewster. "If that cub is still alive," she said, "by God I want to see him."

Deputy Bingham was about to speak when the doctor interrupted them. "Can I talk to the two of you privately?" he asked, motioning them aside.

Libby nodded and walked with him across the room. Brewster followed.

"Josh is much better since we got some food and fluids into him," the doctor said. "But he needs rest desperately. I'm afraid he won't relax as long as he's worried about that cub. It's all he's talked about for the last two hours. I need to know the truth. Is the cub alive?"

"Yes," Brewster said.

"Then I suggest you get him over here as soon as possible."

"Here?" Brewster asked incredulously. "To the hospital?"

The doctor nodded. "I'm keeping Josh a couple of days for observation. But it's going to be a long two days if I have to listen to him rant and rave about that cub the whole time. He's strong enough to go outside for a bit."

Brewster cleared his throat. "Is he strong enough to go to the news conference if we hold it on the front lawn?"

"I would think so; the weather is fine. But he may not be very cooperative."

Brewster gave Libby a tired smile. "Well, it looks like we have an outdoor news conference." He looked at his watch, then rushed over to Josh. "Josh, would you be willing to go outside for a news conference?"

Josh lowered his head without answering.

Libby walked up. "Josh, a lot of people worked hard to find you. They've been worried about you. Don't you think they—"

"I didn't want to be found," Josh said, looking up.

Libby firmed her voice. "Listen. If they hadn't found you last night, you might have died."

"Like Pokey?" Josh said bitterly.

"Oh, Josh. Don't talk that way," Libby pleaded. "I love you, sweetheart." She reached over and gave him a hug. Softly she started crying on his shoulder.

Josh spoke with an exasperated tone. "Mom, please don't cry."

"Would you be up for going outside so I can show you Pokey is okay?" Brewster asked.

Josh failed to look up. "You shot him," he mumbled.

Brewster smiled. "No we didn't. I dare you to go outside. I'll show you I'm not lying."

Still Josh sat motionless.

"Double dare you," Brewster said.

Reluctantly, Josh nodded.

Brewster checked his watch again. "Okay, let's see if Otis will bring them over. I've got some time. I need to get to a phone." He turned and rushed away.

"Where's Dad?" Josh asked.

Libby shook her head sadly. "I don't know. Things

have been pretty rough the last few days." She squeezed Josh's arm, but he stared blankly at the floor. Libby moved quickly around the back of the wheelchair, hiding her tears.

A voice broke the hollow stillness. "Hello, Josh. How are you?"

Libby looked up in surprise, as did Josh. Sam stood awkwardly in the doorway, dressed in clean clothes. His fresh-shaven face and groomed hair looked odd.

Libby stepped around the front of the wheelchair, placing herself between Sam and Josh. She caught her breath and blinked her wet eyes. "Where have you been?" she asked, her voice remote and bitter. "Sleeping off a hangover?"

Sam would not look her in the eyes. He hesitated, then walked slowly forward and squatted beside the wheelchair. "I met with the game warden this morning and told him I shot the cub's mother," Sam said, staring at the floor. "I didn't mean to shoot her. It was an accident. But I was wrong for not admitting it."

Josh looked up, his eyes blinking madly to stop his tears. His words spilled out. "Why did you hit me, Dad? Why did you hit me?"

Sam looked directly at Josh. "Son, have you ever gotten so mad you kicked the wall or something?"

Josh nodded slowly.

Sam continued. "It's not because the wall did anything wrong. It's only that—"

Josh spoke defiantly. "I'm not a wall, Dad."

Sam swallowed hard. "I know you're not. I was just mad at the world, and at myself. I took it out on you, and I was wrong for doing it. I've been Mookee Man."

Josh returned to staring sullenly at his lap.

Sam toyed with the arm of the wheelchair. " . . . I heard on the radio that they found you, but I was afraid that you had . . ." Sam choked on his words and blinked his eyes. "I'm sick," he blurted. "Drinking is just like being sick. I need help."

Josh still refused to look up.

Libby felt no sympathy. This was the same song and dance she'd heard too many times in the last few days. "You won't do anything about it, Sam," she said, her voice cold.

Sam brushed at his eyes with his sleeve. "I already have. I've arranged to leave this afternoon for Missoula. They have an alcohol treatment center there. I'll be gone a month. I know I've got no right, but I'm asking for another chance."

Confused, Libby avoided Sam's eyes. An alcohol treatment center? Was he serious? She grabbed the handles of the wheelchair and started pushing Josh toward the door. "Come on, Josh. We have a news conference to go to."

She expected Sam to rush after her, and to grab her arm and argue. Walking away was the kind of thing that made him blow up at home like a gas can. But as they pushed through the swinging doors, she heard only silence. Josh strained to look back. Finally Libby stole a glance back herself.

Sam knelt on the floor, bent over like a wounded animal. His body jerked with great sobs.

CHAPTER 35

CHAPTER

JOSH HATED seeing his father sob. What was wrong with him? Whatever it was, he should stop.

"Dad," he called. "You're not Mookee Man."

Still his father kneeled on the hospital floor, head and shoulders heaving in spasms. Josh looked up at his mother and saw fear in her eyes. "Mom," he said, "tell Dad he's not Mookee Man so he'll quit cryin'."

His mother trembled, and for a moment Josh thought she might walk away from Sam. But, cautiously, she walked back to him. She reached down and touched his quivering shoulder. "Josh is right," she said. "You're not."

Like a whipped dog, Sam stood, his head hung low. "I am," he said, sobs grabbing at his words. "But I promise when I get back from Missoula, I'll never be Mookee Man again."

Josh watched as his mother lifted Sam's chin and placed a gentle kiss on his drenched cheek. Mom always liked getting mushy. But was there anything that could really change his father? Josh didn't know. Nor was he sure he cared anymore. His body ached, and he felt so weary.

For a moment he had quit thinking about Pokey. But now the thoughts came back, and deep inside the hurt and pain returned. Memories of Pokey nearly choked him. He had failed! Nothing mattered anymore. Who cared if Dad was Mookee Man? Dad could do whatever he wanted. So could Mom. Josh just wanted to be alone. He wanted the whole world to butt out. He'd never forget the cub—never, ever, ever.

"Let's go," his mother said softly, taking Sam's hand. Together they walked up behind Josh and pushed him outside.

Josh squinted into the sun. Several hundred people had gathered on the lawn, cheering and clapping and whistling when they saw him. Three big vans parked in a half circle around the back of the crowd. On top, TV cameras pivoted, following him along the sidewalk. Why were all these people here? What was going on? What was the big deal?

"Josh," Libby said, touching his shoulder lightly.

Josh couldn't hide his curiosity. "What?" he said.

"See, Josh. I told you people were worried about you. Did you know that television stations and newspapers all over the country have been showing your picture?"

Nothing made sense to Josh anymore. Television? Newspapers? What was she talking about? "Why?" he asked.

"Because you did something special."

Josh felt his jaw quiver. "I didn't do anything," he

said. "I just tried to save Pokey . . . but it didn't work. And I think I got Mud Flap killed."

The shouting and cheering drowned out Josh's voice. Officer Bingham stood in front of a small podium, testing a microphone. It squealed and hummed before finally working.

"Ladies and gentlemen," he began. "May I have your attention please. At five o'clock this morning Josh McGuire was located about five miles up Rock Creek. He had been injured in a motorcycle accident. He was brought down to the trailhead, and at six A.M. was transported by helicopter to this hospital for treatment. First I'd like to introduce Dr. Leonard, who will give you an update on his condition. Please hold your questions until we are through."

Somebody still yelled, "Where is the cub?"

Brewster ignored the question and backed away from the podium.

The skinny doctor stepped up to the microphone. "Josh has been through a lot," he said. "He suffered a severe break to the ulna and the radial bone in his left arm and has a laceration on the right upper thigh—this has caused considerable blood loss. He also bruised his ribs. In addition, he has suffered facial and digital frostbite and dehydration. None of these injuries, however, pose any threat. Josh will be released from our hospital within a couple of days, and we expect him to make a full recovery."

The doctor stepped back from the microphone, and people clapped and cheered again. Josh stared at the spectacle. What were they clapping and cheering about? Didn't they know that Pokey and Mud Flap were dead?

Officer Bingham stepped back up to the microphone. "I'd like to say thank you to the Bozeman Search and Rescue members. A few of you still haven't gone home to bed." He motioned toward a group of bedraggled searchers who stood silently to one side of the crowd. Their clothes were dirty and their eyes were hollow from lack of sleep. But each smiled broadly. The crowd broke into applause.

After the clapping died away, Officer Bingham turned back to the crowd. "Last week, many of us here had never heard of Josh McGuire—I for one. But in a short while, his courage has touched a great many lives." He looked over at Josh. "Josh, is there anything you would like to say?" Again the crowd broke into wild clapping and cheers.

Josh wanted to run away from all the cameras and people, but he couldn't. Everyone was looking at him. They acted like this was a big party. Well, it wasn't . . . and yet, there was one thing he did want to say. So he nodded weakly. Officer Bingham brought over the microphone from the podium and held it in front of Josh. The crowd grew quiet except for the clicking and whirring of cameras.

"They killed Pokey! They killed Pokey!" Josh blurted hoarsely.

The crowd murmured loudly. Several people shouted angry questions, but the officer held up his hand for quiet and kept holding the microphone out to Josh. But Josh had said all he intended to say.

Finally the officer gave up and headed back for the podium with the microphone. He spoke into it as he walked, his voice sounding smug. "Well, we'll see about that."

Josh looked up curiously. Was the officer making fun of him? The big man motioned to someone in the back of the crowd, and soon the people spread apart. A man in a suit coat walked forward carrying a small bundle. Coming closer, Josh strained his eyes. It was Mud Flap, all bandaged up but alive.

Behind the man walked Otis. Josh gasped. Otis was carrying Pokey. It couldn't be Pokey. He was dead. Bears didn't have ghosts. Or did they? No—a ghost wouldn't have those button eyes and a plum nose. It wouldn't have that bunny-paw tail and those fuzzy spade ears. It was Pokey!

Suddenly Josh could not contain himself. "Pokey! Mud Flap! Pokey! Mud Flap!" he screamed over and over until the men stopped beside the wheelchair.

The crowd hushed.

First Josh reached over and stroked Mud Flap. "Oh, how you doing, girl? I didn't think you made it."

Mud Flap raised her head, her eyes sparkling. She thumped her tail as the man brought her closer. Josh pressed his head against her muzzle. "Oh, Mud Flap. I won't ever let you get hurt again." He let his hand trail off her hair as the man lowered her to the grass beside the wheelchair. Mud Flap kept wagging her tail, ears perked forward.

Josh looked up at the man. "Who are you?" he asked, distrustfully.

The neatly dressed man smiled warmly. "Son, I'm Governor Cecil Harden."

Josh wasn't sure he believed the man. Why would the governor be here holding Mud Flap? It didn't make sense, nor was it important—Pokey was waiting. Josh looked around.

Otis cradled the cub like a child, rubbing its neck. "Hi, Josh," Otis said.

Josh ignored Otis. "Pokey. I thought they shot you, fella." He reached out.

The cub started clawing to get down. Otis set the big cub awkwardly on Josh's lap. Then he let go of the leash. The cub grunted and sniffed Josh, then clung to his side. Otis turned and followed the governor to the podium.

The cub weighed heavy on Josh's hurt thigh, but it didn't matter. It was Pokey! It was Pokey! He hugged the soft, familiar kinky-haired bundle. He felt the cub tense, then relax in his arms.

Officer Bingham stepped beside the podium and talked quietly with Otis and the governor. Soon Otis returned to the wheelchair. Josh looked up warily at his old friend.

Otis reached down and scratched the cub's back. "How are you doing, Josh?"

Josh hugged the cub, guarding him. "I'm keeping Pokey!"

Otis smiled. "I was hoping you would."

Josh stared in disbelief. "What do you mean? I

thought you said I couldn't? You said they wouldn't let me."

"That's before you stirred up the hornets' nest."

"They're not really going to let me keep him, are they?"

Otis smiled and pointed with his hand to where Officer Bingham was preparing to speak to the crowd again. "Well, maybe this will convince you," he said.

The crowd was hollering questions, and again the officer held up his hand for quiet. "Please, ladies and gentlemen," he said. "Please hold your questions until we're through." He squinted against the midday sun. "Now I'd like to introduce someone you all know . . . Governor Cecil Harden."

The smiling man walked over with a rolling gait. He stopped at the podium and coughed, adjusting his thin tie. The sound of his amplified voice echoed after each word.

"When I went to bed last night in Helena," he started out, "I never dreamed I'd be here in Bozeman this morning talking at a news conference. I have to admit that what this young boy did is a public official's worst nightmare. On the other hand, what he did took courage. After consulting with the head of the State Fish and Game Department, and knowing that this cub has been severely traumatized, I am ordering that he be permanently raised and cared for at a rehabilitation farm."

"I thought you said I could keep him!" Josh whispered angrily to Otis.

Otis raised a finger to his lips and motioned back toward the podium.

Governor Harden turned toward Otis. "Because Otis Sinclair has the proper facilities, I'm turning the cub over to him." At this point the governor looked directly at Josh. "Now it is also my understanding that Mr. Sinclair will soon be a very busy man. For that reason, the care, feeding, and handling of the cub will have to be your responsibility, Josh. Is that something you agree to?"

The words hit Josh like a brick, and he fumbled with his words. "I ah, ah . . . why sure . . . are you kidding? You really mean it?" he cried.

The governor nodded. "As sure as I got out of bed too early this morning."

The crowd burst into applause. Josh looked down at Pokey, but the sound failed to bother the cub. He cuddled closer, pulling a front paw to his nose. Despite the loud clapping, Josh could hear Pokey's deep rhythmic clucking.

Libby turned to Otis. "What did he mean, you'd soon be a busy man?"

Otis fidgeted, then patted Josh's leg. "Well, I figured if a rug rat that can't even start a decent fire can stir things up, maybe I should give it another try."

"I don't understand," Libby said.

Otis cleared his throat. "I've decided to help lobby again for environmental issues at the state capital. It's something I know well, and maybe an old fossil like me can still do some good." Otis turned to Josh.

"And, Josh, I've already warned the governor that the first law I'm taking aim at is the one allowing bears to be hunted—at least in the spring when their cubs are most vulnerable."

"Do you think you can really get them to change that?" Josh asked, choking with surprise.

"Not by myself," Otis said, shaking his head. "Nope, I'll need the help of some celebrities. I was hoping maybe you and Pokey could help me hang those bureaucrats out to dry."

Suddenly Josh smiled big with what his dad would call a coat-hanger-in-the-mouth smile. "Yeah. We'll hang 'em out to dry," he laughed. Then he turned with excitement. "Mom, Dad, did you guys hear that? Did you?"

Libby blinked back her tears and nodded, a smile flooding her face. "I did."

Sam put his arm around Libby, tears glassing his eyes. He smiled weakly, biting at his lip.

Suddenly Josh thought of something. "Otis," he asked. "How is the owl?"

Otis scratched his chin thoughtfully. "Well, I'd say with your help, we might get her flying again."

"Oh, boy," Josh yipped, looking around. Suddenly he froze. What was going on—nobody was shouting or clapping anymore? Cripe, now most everyone was sniffling and dabbing at their eyes—even some of the camera people and the crowd. What a bunch of cry babies.

Josh looked back down at the cub. "You're all mine, Pokey. You're all mine," he said.

Otis reached out and stroked the cub, then squeezed Josh's shoulder lightly. "Josh," he said, "nobody will ever take Pokey away from you. But you have to understand something: Pokey isn't yours."

Josh felt betrayed. "Then you lied," he said stubbornly. "You said I could keep him. That makes him mine."

"Josh, you can't own a wild animal. No one can own a wild animal any more than you can own the clouds or the wind. They belong to themselves. The most you can do is help Pokey and be his friend. Do you understand that?"

Josh blinked, trying to keep his eyes from watering. His eyes always watered in the wind. Trouble was, there was no wind. There was only a wonderful creature clinging tightly to his side. Josh looked down at the black huddled mass for a long time, then nodded and cuddled the cub closer.

AUTHOR'S NOTE
AUTHOR'S NOTE

In 1984, Montana changed its hunting laws to eliminate the spring hunting of bears in Region 3. This included a wide area surrounding Bozeman. This restriction, however, was temporary. As of this writing, spring bear hunting is allowed once again.